Sydney's shoulder muscles screamed in protest as she twisted them into impossible positions, trying desperately to ya~~~~ ~~~~ ~~~~ ~~~~ ~~~~her arms. The air wh~~~~ ~~~~ ~~~~rs to her eyes as she ~~~~ ~~~~gh the thin air, makii~~~~ ~~~~ ~~~~en think.

Just as one of the straps finally slid over her left elbow, a shadow suddenly fell over her from some-where immediately overhead. For a moment she thought it was the plane returning. But a split sec-ond later, she felt a violent yank on the other para-chute strap. She gasped, wanting to shout in protest, but the wind grabbed her words and ripped them away before her ears could register them.

A glance upward confirmed her worst fear . . . she wasn't the only one plummeting toward the ground. She was staring straight into the snarling face of one of the men from the plane—Rabik! Sydney gasped as his elbow connected solidly with her left cheekbone. She felt the parachute slip down her arm as he grabbed for it again. He must have lost his balance during their struggle and fallen out after her.

And now he wanted her parachute. . . .

Don't miss any of the
OFFICIAL ALIAS BOOKS
from Bantam Books

Alias: Declassified
THE OFFICIAL COMPANION

THE PREQUEL SERIES
Recruited
A Secret Life
Disappeared
Sister Spy
The Pursuit/A Michael Vaughn Novel
Close Quarters/A Michael Vaughn Novel
Father Figure
Free Fall
Infiltration
Vanishing Act
Skin Deep

AND COMING SOON
Shadowed

ALIAS™

SKIN DEEP

CATHY HAPKA

AN ORIGINAL PREQUEL NOVEL BASED ON THE HIT TV SERIES CREATED BY J. J. ABRAMS

BANTAM BOOKS

NEW YORK ✶ TORONTO ✶ LONDON ✶ SYDNEY ✶ AUCKLAND

Alias: Skin Deep

A Bantam Book / September 2004
Text and cover art copyright © 2004 by Touchstone Television

ISBN: 0-553-49439-2

Visit us on the Web! www.randomhouse.com

Published simultaneously in the United States and Canada

Bantam Books is an imprint of Random House Children's Books, a
division of Random House, Inc. BANTAM BOOKS and the rooster
colophon are registered trademarks of Random House, Inc.

PRINTED IN THE UNITED STATES OF AMERICA

OPM 10 9 8 7 6 5 4 3 2 1

ALIAS™

SKIN DEEP

"SO TELL ME EVERY little thing about yourself. Every secret."

Sydney Bristow tensed, swallowing back a sudden surge of suspicion and alarm. She forced herself to relax and smile at the tall, good-looking guy who had just leaned closer to her on the park bench. *He's just a UCLA sophomore trying to flirt with me,* she reminded herself. *He's not a spy.*

It was a reminder she had to give herself more and more often as she progressed as an agent-in-training for the CIA. Sometimes it seemed like just yesterday that Wilson had walked up to her on campus and offered her the opportunity of a life-time. At other times she had trouble remembering that she had ever experienced anything resembling "real life"—a life without secret missions that could mean life or death for people all over the planet, a life without lying to everyone she met or escaping from people who were trying to kill her. The experiences she'd had so far in her short career tended to make her a little suspicious of new people.

Still, the logical part of her mind was certain that this college guy was just an ordinary student going about the ordinary business of trying to pick her up. His name was Kent, and she'd met him a few minutes before as she and her best friend and roommate, Francie Calfo, were wandering across the college green debating whether to go for sand-wiches or Chinese for lunch.

Sydney glanced over at Francie, who was standing a few yards away on the grass casually kicking around a Hacky Sack with Kent's friend Carl. Carl was a huge, handsome hunk who was practically drooling all over Francie already. That was Francie—she had a natural allure, a spark that drew guys to her like moths to a flame. Sydney of-ten envied her friend that easy charm and natural friendliness. Francie never seemed to overthink things like Sydney often did. She never seemed to drift off in the middle of a conversation, totally forgetting that the other person wasn't inside her head. . . .

"Well?" Kent leaned still closer, smiling at her. His hand, which had been resting on the wooden bench seat, crept a little closer to her thigh. "Are you going to answer me, or are you playing hard to get?"

Sydney shrugged and forced what she hoped was a playful little laugh. "Oh, there's not much to tell about me, really," she said, tossing her shiny brown ponytail over her shoulder and casually dropping her arm onto the bench between her leg and his hand. "I'm a sophomore, I was born in West Virginia, moved to California, grew up, went off to boarding school. . . ."

"Boarding school, eh?" Kent raised one eyebrow and grinned. "So, like, while the rest of us were stuck in public school and kicking rocks around for fun, you were off at boarding school going to tea parties and horseback riding and playing croquet, right?"

This time Sydney's laugh was real. "Not exactly," she said. "I mean, there was a stable there, so I did go horseback riding once in a while. But the tea and croquet thing? Not so much. I was a total tomboy."

Just then Francie hurried over, dragging her guy by the arm. "Hey, Syd," she blurted out, her dark eyes flashing with excitement. "Carl just invited us to this off-campus party tomorrow night—it's supposed to be totally wild and fun. What do you say? Think we should grace these guys with our fabulous pres—"

Beep! Beep!

Before Francie could finish her sentence, a sharp tone pierced the air. Sydney glanced down at the pager clipped to the waistband of her shorts.

"Oops," she said, flipping the pager up long enough to read the name SLOANE on it. "Sorry."

Francie grimaced and turned away. "Uh-oh," she said in the tight, tense voice she saved for just such occasions. "Sounds like the hive is calling the worker bee again."

Kent looked from Francie back to Sydney in surprise. "You mean you're being called into work on a Saturday?" he exclaimed. "No way. Just blow them off, dude!"

"Oh, she'll never do that," Francie said with a shrug. "She's devoted to her job. Totally."

Sydney bit her lip, fingering the pager. This was

the part of her job she liked the least—lying to the people she cared about. Francie and her other friends didn't know about her secret life as a spy. They all thought that Sydney was a dedicated employee of a bank called Credit Dauphine, which sent her on frequent business trips and corporate retreats. So far, that cover story seemed to do the trick whenever she was called away with only minutes to prepare for the next mission, whether it was just a few miles away in Los Angeles or halfway across the world in Moscow, Paris, or the latest political hot spot. Still, she knew that Francie really didn't understand how a boring bank job could be more important than going to parties, shopping, or just hanging out.

"So are you going to be home for dinner?" Francie asked. "I was going to make something from that cookbook you got me, remember?"

"I—I don't know," Sydney said apologetically, gathering her things from the bench as the lies formed automatically on her tongue. She glanced at Francie. "This page probably has to do with that big project I mentioned the other day. So I'm not sure exactly when I'll be home. I'll let you know, okay?"

"Whatever." Francie shrugged and turned away. "I guess I'll see you later."

Sydney sighed, slinging her bag over her shoulder. She wished she could just ignore the call for once, turn off her pager and enjoy the rest of the pleasant October morning with Francie and the guys like any other college student. She'd been hoping for some downtime from her job ever since returning from the second of two international missions in a row just a couple of weeks earlier. As much as she loved what she did—loved almost everything about it, from the idea of serving her country in such an important way to the rush of adrenaline she got whenever she donned a new disguise and memorized a new alias for a mission— she was really looking forward to catching up on the rest of her life.

But things in the spy business didn't always work that way. There was no way of telling when she would be called away again. Sydney knew that. That didn't mean she had to like it.

"Sorry," Sydney muttered again, lowering her eyes to avoid the all-too-familiar expression of disappointment, resentment, and resignation on Francie's face. "I've really got to go."

* * *

As she hurried into the cool, marble-floored lobby of the Credit Dauphine building, Sydney pushed Francie out of her mind and focused on what was to come. *Maybe they're finally calling me in for debriefing,* she thought, ignoring the usual echoing chatter and commotion going on around her. *Maybe I'm finally going to get some answers about all that Calistrano stuff.*

Her last mission had taken her to England with her frequent partner, a more experienced agent named Noah Hicks. There, she had eventually found herself retrieving mysterious materials from the crypt of a sixteenth-century magician named Calistrano.

Sydney flashed a quick smile at the receptionist as she strode past on her way to the special elevator bank that would take her to sublevel six, where the secret branch of the CIA known as SD-6 had its headquarters. She stared at the doors in front of her as the elevator descended, tapping one foot with barely controlled impatience.

But she wasn't really seeing the smooth metal doors. She was remembering that dank, spooky crypt and thinking about the materials she had found there—information that, according to SD-6's research, could reveal the source of incredible power discovered by Calistrano. But after turning over the material, Sydney had heard nothing more about it. Maybe now she would finally find out if the mission had been as successful as they'd all hoped.

As usual, she felt a brief shiver of anticipation as she stepped out of the elevator and stood in the small, plain entrance room waiting for the retinal scan to identify her. When the door slid open, she hurried through and down the hall, gathering speed as she rounded the corner.

"Heads up!" a male voice warned.

"Oh!" Sydney said breathlessly, skidding to a stop just in time. Her face grew hot as she realized she'd almost crashed right into Noah. She peered up into his ruggedly handsome face, meeting his intense gaze. "Um, hi?"

Though her spy training was helping Sydney become more confident and self-assured by the day, just being around Noah generally made her feel flustered and confused, like a little girl caught at a grown-up party. Noah was only six or seven years older than she was, but sometimes the two of them seemed to come from totally different planets. She was never sure how he would act toward her from one day to the next—sometimes it seemed as though he was as hopelessly attracted to her as she was to him, while at other times he barely seemed to remember she existed. All Sydney knew was that despite it all, she liked being around him. *Really* liked it. She tried not to think too much about it beyond that.

Noah gazed at her with an expression she couldn't quite read. Was he in a good mood? Distracted? Maybe even happy to see her?

"Long time no see," he commented at last, with the smallest hint of a smile. "What's new?"

Sydney laughed, relieved that for once he wasn't putting on a gruff and distant act, as he often did when he saw her at the office. "Not much," she said. "I haven't saved any handcuffed SD-6 agents from secret French tunnels in the past couple of days, if that's what you're wondering."

It was a pretty weak joke—she knew it as soon as the words left her mouth. She also soon realized it was a big mistake. Noah's eyes narrowed, and any hint of a smile faded from his face.

"I *wasn't* wondering that, actually." His voice was cool and deliberate, as though he were giving his order to a particularly slow clerk at a drive-in window. "When you've been doing this as long as I have, perhaps you won't hold on to every little detail of a mission."

Sydney was pretty good at controlling her

emotions—that was part of her training—but she felt herself blushing deeply at Noah's words. *Good one, Syd,* she told herself sharply. *Way to ruin the moment, as usual.*

Noah was so tough and seasoned as a spy, not to mention competitive by nature. She should have known he wouldn't be amused by her joking reference to their first mission in Paris, when she had found him handcuffed to a steel ring on the floor in an underground room. She'd been reminiscing about that mission as she realized she had marked a full year at SD-6, and somehow her recent thoughts had slipped from her lips.

"You're probably right," she muttered, not sure whether to feel more annoyed with Noah or herself. "Anyway, I was just paying you back for saving me before that. Now if you'll excuse me, I have someplace to be right now."

"Me too," Noah muttered back, stepping aside to let her pass. "In fact, I'm late for a very important meeting."

"Fine. See you later, then."

Sydney hurried off down the hall. She was painfully aware of Noah's footsteps directly behind her, and waited impatiently for them to peel off through a doorway or down a different hall.

Instead, he stayed right behind her as she turned

corners and passed through doorways. Sydney was hyperaware of his footsteps and even his breathing, which she could hear even over the soft whir of computers and other equipment as she passed office cubicles and computer labs. She felt her muscles tensing and an anxious twitch starting somewhere in her throat. Was he messing with her?

Finally she whirled around. "Why are you following me?" she exclaimed. "Can't you find a different way to get wherever you're going?"

Noah scowled at her. "Not really," he said, gesturing toward the other end of the hall. "Sloane's office is right down there."

"Sloane's office?" Sydney blinked. "But that's where I'm going." She belatedly realized what that meant. Of course—if this was a debriefing, Noah would have to be there, too. "So maybe we're finally going to find out what all that Calistrano business was all about," she commented, hoping to make amends for her outburst.

"Maybe." Noah brushed past her. "And maybe if we don't stand around here yapping, we won't both be late."

Sydney sighed. She followed him into the spacious, well-appointed office of Arvin Sloane, Sydney's handler and a very important person at SD-6.

Several people were already seated at a conference

table at one end of the room. Sydney nodded a greeting to the other agents, most of whom she had met previously. Then she took a seat beside Graham Flinkman, the resident SD-6 techie.

"Hey, Sydney," Graham greeted her. As usual he sounded so eager and enthusiastic that his voice almost trembled, as if relieved to escape safely from his throat. "How's it going?"

"Great," Sydney replied distractedly with a sidelong glance at Noah, who had just sat down at the other end of the table. "Just great."

Before Graham could say anything else, an interior door opened and a man stepped through. Immediately, the entire room fell silent.

Arvin Sloane wasn't a big man—in fact he was rather slight, with soft features and silver hair that made him look older than he was. But his presence filled any room he entered.

"Good morning," he greeted the others, taking a seat in the large leather chair at the head of the table. "I'm glad you're all here; we have some important business to discuss."

Sydney smiled and leaned forward. *This is it,* she thought. *This is when we find out what that last crazy mission was all about. What we risked our lives for.*

Sloane turned to meet her gaze. "Sydney," he said abruptly. "You know how to ride a horse, right?"

Sydney blinked, startled by the unexpected question. "Well—well, sure, I guess," she said, slightly unnerved by having Sloane's cool, intelligent gaze focused so intently on her. "I mean, I rode some at boarding school. I wouldn't say I was great at it or anything—I probably only rode once a week at the most—but I didn't usually fall off or anything, and, um . . ."

She knew she was babbling. Taking a deep breath, she forced herself to stop. She nodded briskly to clarify her answer to the question.

"Good," Sloane said, as if he hadn't noticed her long-winded response. He glanced around the room. "We have an important new mission," he said. "And Sydney will be going undercover."

Sydney leaned back in her chair, dismay and excitement suddenly fighting it out in the pit of her stomach. Despite the danger, the long hours, and the constant uncertainty, each new mission she completed made her feel more confident. Her new life as a spy was almost addicting, and even after such a short time with SD-6 she couldn't imagine what kind of person she would be without it. But how was she going to explain another sudden absence to Francie, especially so soon after the last one?

From across the room she caught Noah's eye. *Giddyup,* he mouthed.

2

"AARGH! HOW DOES ANYBODY ever get these stupid things on?"

Sydney yanked the tall, black leather boot off her foot in frustration, tossing it halfway across the hotel room. It hit the opposite wall with a satisfying thunk.

". . . and yesterday, in Sydney . . ."

At the sound of her name Sydney jumped, then glanced toward the TV in consternation. She had arrived in Sydney, Australia, just an hour earlier, and was having trouble getting used to hearing her name every time she turned around. At the moment a reporter was reading off the morning news, and the name Sydney seemed to pop up just about every other word.

Sydney changed the channel to a children's cartoon. *Tammy Rae Fielding,* she reminded herself. *My name is Tammy Rae Fielding now.* She glanced across the room at the crumpled shape that was her boot. *And Tammy Rae Fielding wears riding boots all the time. So I'd better figure out how to get that one on my foot.*

Standing up, she hobbled over and retrieved the boot. Her thigh muscles still ached from the intensive remedial riding lessons Sloane had arranged for her before she left the United States. And the fifteen-hour flight to Australia had helped stiffen both of her legs into swollen, knotty masses of soreness that protested every time she moved. Sydney glanced toward the half-open bathroom door, wishing she had time to soak in a nice, hot bath. Instead, she realized she needed to hurry—she was supposed to meet Noah in his room next door in ten minutes.

She decided to try pulling on the boot from a standing position. She maneuvered herself into what seemed like a likely position, with the boot on the edge of the bed and her foot poised over it. She carefully slid her toes into the top, grabbing the edges of the boot tops as her foot met resistance near the ankle section. Feeling one of her long, fake red fingernails bend back, she grimaced and loosened her grip. Sydney always kept her nails at a practical length, but for some reason Tammy Rae seemed to need inch-long scarlet claws on every finger.

Readjusting her grasp on the boot, Sydney yanked as hard as she could, grunting and groaning as her foot jammed in the narrow passage of stiff leather. She was bending over for another pull, her rear end high in the air, when . . .

"Ready to go?"

Sydney lost her balance and toppled over, her boot skidding under the bed as she landed on one hip on the carpeting. She turned to glare at Noah, who was standing in the doorway between their adjoining rooms with a smug grin on his face.

"Very funny," Sydney muttered, leaning over to retrieve her boot. "I know we're supposed to blend in here and everything, but I think the Australians believe in that quaint little tradition of knocking before you enter someone's room, just like we do back in the States."

Noah raised one craggy eyebrow. "Nice accent, Tammy Rae," he said. "One would almost think you were from California instead of Texas."

"Sorry, hon," Sydney said, overloading every syllable with a syrupy Southern accent. "This better, y'all?" She waggled one fake fingernail in his face. "By the way, I don't think that's the proper way for a servant to talk to his employer, now, do you, hon?"

Noah's smile faded, and Sydney hid her own grin. She couldn't help being amused that Noah's alias on this mission was James Marks, Tammy Rae's longtime and loyal servant. Despite his experienced professionalism, she could tell it got under his skin to have to play that kind of role—especially with her.

"Enough chitchat," Noah said with a scowl. "We're not here for fun and games—we need to get organized. Do you have the stuff Graham cooked up?"

"Right over there." Sydney gestured toward the array of clothing and other objects strewn on the bed. Most of it looked like ordinary clothes or riding equipment, but the everyday items hid all sorts of useful spy gadgets—a slender, deadly blade hidden in a riding crop, a camera built into a belt buckle, and more.

"All right. We should head over to the event grounds and scope them out," Noah said. "But let's go over our story one more time first. After that long flight, we don't want to get confused."

Sydney frowned, guessing that the "we" was really referring to her. "You don't have to worry about that," she said sharply. "I know the drill. My cover story is that I'm an American nouveau riche who's shopping for a new competition horse at the three-day event that's taking place here this weekend. I've only been riding for a couple of years, and dabbling with eventing for even less time, which means I've got more money than skill."

She was relieved by that part of the story, since it meant she didn't have to ride *well*—just well enough. Even after her recent intensive review of her riding skills, she wasn't sure she could do much better than stay on the horse.

"Right," Noah said. "We're supposed to—"

"I'm supposed to try out some horses for sale and befriend one of the competitors in the event," Sydney went on, interrupting him. "Her name is Melanie Lawton, and one of her top horses is for sale. She also happens to be the daughter of Australian billionaire Miles Lawton. Our mission is to get close to Lawton through his daughter, to try to find out if SD-6's suspicions about him are right— they think he may be funding some of the world's deadliest terrorist groups in Malaysia and Eastern Europe, among other sneaky, nasty things." She paused, shooting Noah a slightly smug look.

"Right," Noah drawled, seeming unimpressed. "But don't forget—Tammy Rae doesn't know anything about Miles Lawton. She's never even heard of him. So you don't want to mention him until Melanie does."

"I'll try to keep that fact in my feeble brain," Sydney said, going for a joking tone and failing completely. She glared at Noah in annoyance.

Sloane said this was my mission, she thought. *Noah is just supposed to be here as my backup. So why is he trying to take over already?*

She took a deep breath, realizing almost immediately that she was overreacting. Maybe that long flight had taken more out of her than she'd realized. She needed to chill out and remember why she was there—to complete an important mission, *not* to argue with Noah.

Meanwhile, Noah stepped over to pick up the black-velvet-covered riding helmet lying on the bed. He examined it carefully. Both he and Sydney knew that it contained a small but extremely sensitive digital recorder complete with an amplifier for eavesdropping on the quietest of conversations. At the op-tech meeting, Graham had proudly explained that the recorder also included a filter that would screen out all extraneous ambient noise—and that the helmet had been specially custom-fitted to Sydney's head and covered in the most elegant Italian velvet.

"You know, that Graham is good." Noah's deep voice lowered slightly in admiration. "Really good. Have to admit, I was a little skeptical when Sloane said he's the best op-tech guy we've ever had. But I'm starting to think he's right. Graham might be a little odd, but he's got the touch with this stuff."

As he set the helmet back on the bed, Sydney felt another flare of annoyance. How could Noah do that? One moment the two of them were sniping at each other, and a moment later he was chatting casually about op-tech and acting as if nothing had ever happened.

"Okay, I agree, Graham is a genius," she said, leaning over and finally pulling on her boot with one more determined yank. She winced as she felt the stiff leather dig into the skin at her ankles, but she ignored the pain. "I just hope he built some head protection into that helmet along with all the superspy stuff. I may need it when I try to ride that horse of Melanie's."

"I'm sure you'll be fine," Noah said.

Sydney shrugged, rocking back and forth on

her heel as she tried to get used to the constricting feel of the boot. "At least one of us is sure," she muttered, feeling the familiar tingle of premission jitters coupled with a healthy dose of extra nervousness. "You do know what eventing is all about, right? They go jumping around a cross-country course over huge, solid stuff, like giant logs and rock walls and stuff. Everyone says the horses *and* the riders are all a little crazy. Total adrenaline-fueled nutcases."

Noah smiled, the weather-beaten skin at the corners of his eyes crinkling a little. "Good," he said. "Then you should fit right in."

Before Sydney could figure out if that was a compliment, an insult, or just a joke, Noah checked his watch.

"Got a date?" Sydney quipped.

"No, but you do," Noah replied. "With Melanie Lawton, to try that horse. We're supposed to meet her at the event grounds in less than two hours."

"Don't worry," Sydney assured him. "It shouldn't take me that long to get my second boot on." She grabbed the boot and shoved her foot into it, doing her best not to grimace with pain as she yanked at the stiff leather.

"Is your signaling device still in place?" Noah tapped his cheek. "I just double-checked mine."

Sydney nodded, glancing down at her fake fingernails. Set into the red lacquer coating her left thumbnail was a tiny rhinestone—or at least, that was what it looked like. It was really a miniature transmitter that would allow Noah to track her position if necessary. Noah had one, too, except that his had been disguised as a filling in one of his teeth.

"Should we test them, just in case?" she asked, her right hand poised to flick the rhinestone and set off the signal.

"No!" Noah barked, taking a quick step toward her. "Remember what Graham said—anyone with similar technology will be able to pick up the signals if they happen to be listening. That's why we're to use the devices only in an emergency."

"Right," Sydney said, feeling slightly foolish. She was getting better at this spy business all the time, but Noah seemed to have a knack for reminding her that she still had a lot to learn.

If Noah noticed her consternation, he didn't let on. "We're going to have to be careful here. Sloane said there are likely to be operatives from other groups tracking Lawton. According to intel our guys have intercepted, Miles Lawton seems to be up to something big."

"But no one can figure out exactly what it is," Sydney finished for him with a shiver of nervous excitement. "That's why it's so important for us to get close to him."

"Yes. But the most important thing is to be careful." Noah took another step closer, his gaze fixed on her face. "You have a difficult role to play here, and when we're dealing with a guy like Lawton, things could get very dangerous very fast. And this is just a surveillance mission. I don't want you to take unnecessary risks . . ."

Sydney caught her breath. Was he saying what she thought he was saying? After all they'd been through together, was he actually starting to worry about her safety?

". . . and we don't to blow this mission, or it could be impossible to find out anything useful about Lawton in the future."

She sighed. She should have known. "So let's get going," she said, ducking her head to hide her emotions. She slipped back into her Southern drawl. "Time's a-wastin', sugar."

She grabbed the helmet from the bed and tucked the riding crop into her back pocket. She quickly checked her reflection in the mirror over the dresser and tried not to wince at the enormous hairdo of her blond wig or the rather garish makeup she'd applied earlier. She suspected she didn't have to worry about anyone recognizing her in her Tammy Rae getup—she barely recognized herself.

"Ready?" she asked Noah.

"Almost. Be right back."

As Noah slipped back into his room, Sydney checked the time and did a quick calculation. It was about four o'clock in the afternoon back in California. Sydney pulled out the tiny secured-line cell phone she always carried with her and dialed Francie's number.

"'Lo?" a sleepy voice answered after five or six rings.

"Francie? Did I wake you?"

Sydney heard her friend yawn through the phone. "Sort of. I got in late last night—was just taking a nap."

"That off-campus party?" Sydney felt a twinge. Jealousy? Regret? She and her roommate had been so close for the first few months of school—the months before Sydney had joined SD-6—that it was always a little weird when Francie did something without her, even when it was Sydney's schedule that was to blame. "Fun?"

"Yeah."

Sydney smiled. She knew that tone—it meant that her friend had met yet another guy at the party.

"Can't wait to hear the details. Promise to fill me in when I get back?"

"Of course." Francie was sounding more awake all the time. "How's your dad?"

"A little better." The lie slipped out so easily, so naturally and smoothly. Sydney had called Francie as soon as she'd found out about her new mission, planting her cover story by saying that she'd had a call at work that her father had fallen ill. A few hours later she'd called again to say that he had taken a turn for the worse and she was driving up to take care of him.

The cover story had been Sloane's idea, and Sydney hadn't been sure it would work. Ever since Sydney's mother had died in a car accident when Sydney was only six, father and daughter just didn't seem to have anything in common aside from their grief, which they dealt with in their own ways. Jack Bristow had buried himself in his work selling airplane parts, while Sydney had learned to get along mostly on her own. Francie knew the whole story, and Sydney had wondered whether her friend would believe that her father had asked her to come take care of him. But Francie had accepted the tale in her usual sympathetic, caring way, not seeming the least bit suspicious.

That's just because she doesn't know Dad like I

do, Sydney thought with a brief grimace. *Truth is, if he got sick, I'd probably be the last person he wanted to see. I'd be lucky if he even remembered to call and let me know.*

Realizing that Francie was still waiting, she cleared her throat. "Anyway, I think I'd better stick around here a few more days at least. He still can't get around too well, and he asked if I could stay."

"Sure, I understand. And I'm so glad you and your dad are finally connecting, even if it took something like this to bring you together." Francie paused. "Oh, and Syd . . . sorry I was so harsh on you the other day on the green. You know, when you got called into work? If I'd known this was going to happen . . . Forgive me?"

"Of course." Sydney smiled into the phone, once again feeling the familiar twinge of guilt that swept through her whenever she lied to Francie. "Don't even worry about it. Thanks for understanding."

"No biggie," Francie said. "Take your time, and do what you have to do. My best healing vibes are going out to your dad."

"Thanks." Sydney heard the door swing up. She glanced up to see Noah walking back into the room. "Listen, Francie, I'd better go. I'll call you when I can, okay?"

3

"JAMES! THE ICE IN my drink is melting. Could you be a dear and fetch me a few fresh cubes from the soda stand?"

Sydney smiled brightly at Noah. Several people nearby turned and watched curiously as Noah shot her a brief, almost imperceptible glare before hurrying toward the row of snack booths set up along the gravel path leading toward the main competition areas. Sydney could tell she was attracting attention with her loud Texan drawl, but that was okay. Unlike many of her aliases, Tammy Rae wasn't really supposed to blend into the scenery.

Sydney looked around curiously. It was mid-morning, but the event grounds were already busy. She and Noah had arrived about ten minutes earlier and were still wandering around getting their bearings. Sydney was keeping her eyes peeled for any sign that there were other operatives doing the same thing, but so far she hadn't spotted any likely suspects. It was the first day of the three-day event, and riders were running around frantically preparing for their dressage tests, while spectators headed toward the ring to watch the tests, strolled around the inviting grounds, or visited the food and merchandise tents clustered near the entrance. Aside from a loose dog sniffing furtively at an unguarded lunch cooler, nobody looked the least bit suspicious.

Of course, we shouldn't expect enemy operatives to skulk around wearing dark sunglasses and I Hate America patches on their trench coats, Sydney reminded herself. *They'll be undercover, just like we are.*

She glanced around, realizing that their enemies could be anywhere. That woman dabbing at a spot on her white breeches could be a member of Mercado de Sangre. Or that older man in the Bermuda shorts and black socks snapping pictures of the pretty horses might be a K-Directorate agent, and thus an enemy of SD-6. One thing Sydney had already learned in her brief career as a spy was never to take anything for granted. It just wasn't always easy to remember that.

A moment later Noah returned, holding a paper cup full of ice. Sydney held up her own cup. "Thank you so much, James dear," she cooed loudly, fanning herself with her free hand. "Why, I don't know how I'm ever going to get used to this dry heat."

"Let's not go overboard with this stuff, okay?" Noah growled into her ear as he bent over her to plop the ice cubes into the drink she was holding.

Sydney bit back a grin. "Hey, I'm just staying in character . . . *James,*" she murmured back.

"Fine," Noah said through gritted teeth. "But look, we still have almost an hour before we're supposed to meet Melanie Lawton. Why don't we split up for a while? We'll be able to get more recon done that way."

Sydney suspected that efficient recon wasn't the only reason he wanted to get away from her for a while. But she realized he had a point.

"Okay," she said. "Let's meet at Melanie's barn in an hour."

* * *

A little while later Sydney was wandering through the busy grounds trying to look like she fit in. She had left the food and shopping area and wandered past the warm-up ring. Just beyond that, she saw a crowd gathered at the top of a hill. She walked toward them, eventually finding herself at the main ring. Most of the spectators were seated on the temporary bleachers set up along one side of the ring, but Sydney found an empty spot on the opposite side and watched as a tall, thin man entered riding a lean gray gelding.

Sydney didn't have much firsthand experience with dressage—back in boarding school, her instruction had been in hunt seat. But from her premission study, she knew that it was the first of three phases of a three-day event. While the cross-country and show-jumping phases sounded exciting, the dressage—a strictly circumscribed pattern intended to test the horse's training and obedience, conducted on the flat in a small, rectangular ring—had sounded a little boring to her. But now, watching the gray and its rider perform, she found herself fascinated.

Sydney had always been observant by nature, and thanks to her intensive spy training, she was good at spotting even the smallest details. But she had trouble seeing any movement in the rider, any signal he might be giving the horse—it was as if man and horse were reading each other's minds, the animal turning this way and that or changing gait according to a sort of natural synthesis, each movement leading smoothly into the next. Sydney found herself smiling in appreciation. It reminded her a little bit of her own line of work—spies often had to depend on all sorts of nonverbal communication, taking their cues from people's facial expressions, their every twitch or blink or quiver, like a secret dance. . . .

Finally the horse and rider came to a brisk, square halt on the center line facing the judges' stand. The crowd broke into polite applause as the rider completed his salute, and the sound snapped Sydney out of her reverie. She realized that time was passing while she stood there focused on the dancing horse. Good thing Noah hadn't happened by and seen her.

With one last glance at the gray and its rider, she turned and wandered on, trying to look like a slightly bored tourist in search of something new to see. After strolling past the far end of the ring and down a nicely landscaped dirt path, she came upon a cluster of large canvas tents that made up the temporary stabling for the competitors. Peering into the first tent, she saw that the airy space inside held double rows of pipe stalls. Inside most of them, horses were eating, pacing, snoozing, or staring into space.

Sydney moved on to the next set of tents, glancing into each one as she passed. Even after all of her training and her previous missions, it was a little hard for her to imagine that there could be enemy agents in such a bucolic place. She stepped out of the way as a groom hurried past her with a gleaming bay horse in tow. It jigged nervously on the end of its line, every muscle in its fit, rangy body outlined beneath its taut, glossy coat. The horse tossed its head, then glanced in her direction and let out a loud, sudden snort.

I hope I can pull this off, Sydney thought with an uncomfortable twinge of self-doubt as she watched the horse prance off. *The horses I used for those practice rides didn't look quite like these guys. . . .*

She bit her lip. The idea of spying on international criminals and possibly tangling with enemy agents didn't really make her that nervous anymore—she was well trained to handle that sort of thing. But climbing aboard a horse that might not appreciate her novice attempts to ride it? *That* made her nervous.

She glanced at the people standing nearby.

None of them looked particularly concerned with the horses passing back and forth. Sydney wasn't sure whether that made her feel better or not.

A pair of teenage girls wandered past, chatting to a slender young woman leading yet another fit, alert horse into the stabling area. The horse cast a suspicious eye at a tent flap waving weakly in a breeze and scooted a few steps to the side. But neither the woman nor the girls seemed to notice as they walked on.

See? Sydney told herself. *Even the kids around here act like these horses are no more trouble than the average golden retriever. If they can relax, I can too. I have to, or people might get suspicious of my— Hey, wait a minute. . . .*

Another figure had just come into view, a man who seemed to belong neither to the crowds of slim, tanned riders nor the smiling spectators. He was a big man, squarely built, with shoulders like cement blocks beneath his dark suit, and a hard, alert face.

Lawton, Sydney thought eagerly, recognizing the man from photos she had seen back at SD-6 HQ. *It's Lawton!*

This was a lucky break—they hadn't known whether Lawton would be attending the event to watch his daughter ride. Controlling her excitement, Sydney forced her gaze away from him. The last thing she wanted to do was blow the mission when it had hardly begun by making Lawton notice her. But she also didn't want to miss this chance to learn more.

As Lawton strode purposefully down the wide dirt path between two rows of tents, Sydney kept track of him in her peripheral vision. She pretended to check the time, then drifted casually after him, trying to look like she was just sightseeing. There were enough people in the stabling area that she was able to keep him in sight easily, leaving just a few people between them as she followed him down several more rows of tents. Luckily, he didn't turn around or even glance left or right, seeming intent on reaching his destination—wherever that was.

He's probably just going to wish Melanie well or something, Sydney realized as she dodged a sweaty horse receiving a bath in the aisle just in time to see Lawton turn the corner at the end of the row. *I'll have to make sure she doesn't see me if that's the case—don't want to raise any suspicions.*

She rounded the corner and saw that the canvas tent stalls had come to an end and she was facing several parallel rows of long, wooden barns. There were fewer people back here, though she could hear the occasional nicker, snort, or stomp of a horse inside. Lawton had slowed his pace and seemed to be checking the numbers painted on the barn doors. Sydney dropped back a little. She was still carrying her riding helmet, and she quickly set it on her head and pulled the brim down as low as it would go. That way, she hoped she would just look like another passing rider if he saw her.

Finally he turned and entered a barn at the end of the row. Sydney strolled up to the entrance, trying to look natural. But a quick glance around showed her that the area was completely deserted. Hurrying forward and taking a deep breath, she peeked into the darkened barn entrance. Lawton was inside, looking into a stall a few yards down the aisle with his back to the door. Two other men were standing beside him, and indecipherable sounds of quiet conversation drifted toward Sydney.

She darted inside and scooted behind a stack of hay bales near the door, ducking down to hide herself in case the men should turn around. The sweet scent of the hay tickled her nose, and she swallowed a sneeze. Then she craned her neck, peering over the top bale.

The men were still engrossed in their conversation. Sydney could see that the second man was shorter than Lawton and much thinner, with sandy brown hair and glasses. The third man was paunchy and balding, with ruddy skin and a moon face.

Pictures, Sydney realized. *I should take pictures—we can send them to Graham, and he can try to ID the other two men.*

She glanced down, realizing that her belt buckle camera was going to be pretty much useless in her hiding place unless she stood on her head. Thinking fast, she glanced around and spotted a vertical gap between the stacks of bales. Scooting over, she squatted down behind it. The gap was only about six inches wide, but the three men were just visible through it. Doing her best to aim the belt camera through the gap, Sydney snapped several pictures. Considering the conditions, she wasn't sure whether the images would be clear enough to do any good, but she figured it was the best she could do without giving away her position.

The men were still holding a murmured conversation. Remembering the amplifier in her helmet, Sydney reached for the strap buckle and used her fingernail to press the almost invisible power button. Sydney winced as the sensitive speakers built into the helmet's satin lining immediately picked up every sound in about a fifty-yard radius. Within a split second, though, the carefully calibrated instruments filtered out the extra noise—horses moving their hooves in the straw, a bird singing somewhere just outside the barn, the distant sound of the PA system—to leave only the men's voices. Sydney peeked over the top bale again as she listened.

". . . do you think?" Lawton's rumbling voice was asking. "This gelding a likely candidate?" He gestured into the stall in front of him. By squinting, Sydney could just make out the outline of a dark-colored horse inside.

The shorter man shrugged. "I'm a vet, not a customs official, mate," he replied. "But the scar shouldn't show much on this one, if that's what you mean. Lot easier to hide than it would be on your daughter's gray."

The third man spoke up. "Still think we ought to grab that one, too," he said. "There's real interest in that gelding—my connections would have no trouble doing up a deal for him. Would make the whole batch look better."

"We've already discussed this." Lawton's voice was icy. "The gray is out. End of story. Now, Doctor, how long will the operation take you?"

"Not long, once I have what I need."

"Good." Lawton nodded and glanced at the third man, who shrugged but remained silent. "Let's give it a burl, then. I'll be in touch—we'll have to arrange to get you the drum you need for this horse and the others."

The horse wandered to the front of the stall and stuck its head out, snuffling at the men curiously. The vet reached out to give the animal a pat on the nose, but Lawton and the other man merely stepped away, paying it no attention at all.

Sydney stared at the horse, wondering what was going on. Was there something special about this particular animal? She had heard of horses being injected with drugs and other substances to affect their performances in various competitions—was that what the men were plotting? Perhaps Lawton wanted to give his daughter an extra advantage at the big event.

No, Sydney decided almost immediately. *If Lawton is everything SD-6 thinks he is, he's not going to risk drawing attention for something so unimportant in the grand scheme of things . . . but then, what could that horse possibly have to do with international terrorism?*

It just didn't make sense. The whole situation left Sydney feeling confused and a little frustrated. She scooted a little farther down the barn aisle, staying carefully behind the stacks of hay. Maybe if she could take a look around the rest of the barn . . . The aisle was shadowy and dim, illuminated only by small puddles of sunlight coming through the dusty windows of the front wall. The men were all watching the horse again now; they didn't so much as glance in Sydney's direction as she peered out from behind the end bale. Taking a deep breath, she darted out of the shelter of her hiding place and glided across the aisle and around the corner at the end of the row of stalls.

She was still smiling with relief as she turned around—and almost tripped over a large wheelbarrow loaded with manure and soiled straw. "Oy!" the girl on the other side of the wheelbarrow exclaimed, her voice exploding through Sydney's helmet speakers. "Heads up—don't want to tip this all over your nice clean breeches."

"Sorry," Sydney muttered, keeping her voice as low as possible as she quickly reached up and switched off the amplifier.

"No worries," the girl responded cheerfully, her voice still ringing all too loudly through the barn. "Can I help you with something? You lost?"

Sydney shook her head and forced her best Tammy Rae smile. "No, thanks, hon," she said. "I just came in here following my bracelet—the darn thing rolled all the way in here from outside, and I guess I got a little turned around." She held up her left arm and jingled the gold bracelets she'd slipped on earlier as part of her disguise.

"Oh. Fine, then." The girl seemed satisfied with the answer. She pointed back in the direction Sydney had come. "Exit's out that way."

"Susan?" a man's voice called from around the corner. "Who are you talking to over there?"

The girl with the wheelbarrow glanced toward the voice. "Nobody, boss," she called back. "Just someone passing through."

Sydney recognized the voice as belonging to the third man who had been standing with Lawton and the vet. "I'd better go," she told the girl. "Don't want to get y'all in any trouble."

She heard several sets of footsteps coming down the aisle and estimated that she only had a few seconds before the men rounded the corner and saw her standing there. *I can't blow this,* she told herself. *If Lawton and his cronies see me . . .*

Still, she forced herself to walk at a moderate speed—like a wealthy woman fleeing a potentially embarrassing situation, rather than a spy fearing exposure. She took a few steps toward the front of the barn, but she had just spotted a back exit at the other end of the short side aisle. As soon as Susan turned away to pick up the handles of her wheelbarrow, Sydney spun around and darted out the back door. Blinking against the bright sunlight outside, she hurried away at a brisk jog. She didn't slow down and glance back until she was safely mixing with the crowds at the end of the stable row. Only then did she let out a sigh of relief. Turning and scanning the area she'd just left from behind a handy Porta-Potti, she saw the third man standing outside the barn looking around. After a moment he shrugged and disappeared back inside.

Sydney let out a sigh of relief. Checking her watch, she realized it was almost time to meet Noah. She would have to hurry to make it to Melanie's barn in time—especially since she had no idea where it was.

LUCKILY, THE VERY FIRST person Sydney asked knew exactly where Melanie Lawton's horses were stabled and was happy to point Sydney in the right direction. It turned out to be quite close by in one of the canvas tents Sydney had passed earlier, and she ended up arriving with plenty of time to spare. She glanced inside at the row of temporary stalls, wondering which of the elegant, athletic horses looking back at her was the one she would be riding.

Not wanting to think about that until she had to, she wandered out to the end of the stable row and looked around. A hard-packed dirt path led off in the direction of the competition areas, and on the far side of the path was a fenced riding ring where a man was lunging a handsome chestnut.

Sydney bought herself a bottle of water at a nearby food booth and stood against the ring's wooden fence. She watched the horse trot along at the end of the long lunge line, doing her best to hide her impatience as she waited for Noah.

He strolled up the dirt path about thirty seconds ahead of their prearranged time. Spotting her immediately, he walked toward her.

"James!" Sydney cried, careful to use her best Tammy Rae accent. "There you are, sugar. I've been looking everywhere for you." She shot him a meaningful look.

"Sorry, miss," Noah said. Then he leaned closer. "What's up?" he added in a low tone.

"I saw Lawton," Sydney whispered back.

"Is she here already?" Noah glanced around expectantly.

Sydney shook her head. "No, not Melanie—Miles," she told him.

Noah's expression sharpened instantly. "Tell me."

"He's here on the show grounds," Sydney said as the two of them turned and walked slowly in the direction of Melanie's stalls. "I recognized him from photos and tailed him to some barns at the back of the stabling area. He met up with two other men there, and they talked about a particular horse."

"A horse?" Noah raised an eyebrow. "What do you mean?"

Sydney shrugged. "That seemed a little weird to me, too," she admitted. "But they definitely didn't want to be seen. Considering who Lawton is, I think we should assume he was up to no good."

"Well, that much is true enough." Noah glanced around to make sure no one was listening to their conversation. "I talked to a few people just now about him—grooms and such. Every one of them seemed to truly adore Melanie, but most of them got a little less happy when I brought up her father's name."

"Did you find out anything about what he's up to?"

"Not really. At least, not anything that seems to relate to our mission. Just that he's been buying quite a few good horses over the past few months."

"For Melanie to ride?"

Noah shook his head. "Seems he's become a horse trader of sorts," he said. "He buys good horses in Australia and New Zealand and resells them to friends in Europe."

"Cover business for something else?" Sydney guessed.

"Probably," Noah agreed.

Before either of them could say anything else, a young woman hurried toward them. She had a pretty, heart-shaped face scattered with freckles. Her straight blond hair was pulled back into a short, neat ponytail, and she was neatly though not elegantly dressed in faded black breeches and a T-shirt.

"G'day," she said brightly. "Are you the American buyer who's come to have a look at my mare? I'm Melanie Lawton. My mates call me Mel, so you should too."

Sydney smiled, liking the young woman's open, friendly manner immediately. "Hi there, sugar," she said, holding out her hand. "I'm Tammy Rae Fielding, from Texas. It's so lovely to meet y'all. Oh—this is my personal assistant, James." She gestured toward Noah, who bowed his head slightly in greeting.

"So nice to meet you both," Melanie said sincerely. "Want to get right to it, then? Come along. Good old Rocket is back this way."

"Rocket?" Sydney couldn't help feeling a flash of alarm at the name. "Er, I thought the horse's name was Smooth Sailing."

"That's her show name," Melanie explained with a mischievous wink. "But around the barn, we just call her Rocket. Or sometimes Butthead—if she's being especially good that day." She laughed.

Sydney did her best to join in. Out of the corner of her eye, she caught Noah smirking. Shooting him a dirty look, she turned to follow Melanie into the canvas barn.

Melanie led them to a stall near the end of the aisle. "This is her," she said as a very tall, very lean chestnut horse with a distinctive crooked blaze looked out at them. "She's a silly old thing, but we'll be sorry to see her go."

Sydney could tell that Melanie was genuinely fond of the chestnut mare, which made her feel slightly better about what she was supposed to do. But only slightly.

"Er—is she very spirited?" Sydney patted Rocket gingerly on the neck as Melanie pulled a carrot chunk out of a pocket and fed it to the horse. "That is, as y'all know, I haven't been doing this very long, and, well . . ."

"Yes, I understand," Melanie broke in with a nod. "I won't say she's an old plug by any means— wouldn't make much of an eventer if she was, right? But she's dead honest over fences and loves her job. She can get a bit enthusiastic at times, but she means well, really. I'm sure you'll be able to handle her just fine."

Sydney wasn't quite so sure. But she wasn't about to blow the mission over a few preride jitters. "Great," she said with as much enthusiasm as she could muster. "She sounds like a fun horse."

"Oh, she is that," Melanie assured her. "Just give me a sec, and I'll get her tacked up for a test ride."

Noticing that Noah still looked a little too amused by the whole situation, Sydney smiled innocently at Melanie. "Just let James know if y'all need help with anything," she said. "He's here to serve."

"Thanks," Melanie said. "But I should be okay. Why don't you wait out by the schooling ring? We'll be out shortly."

Sydney and Noah wandered back outside to the ring. The chestnut was gone, but there were several other horses now warming up or schooling, and a number of people were leaning on the fence watching them and occasionally calling out advice to their riders. Sydney took a few deep breaths, trying to calm the butterflies in the pit of her stomach.

Noah leaned beside her, glancing at her face. "Ready for this?" he asked in a low voice.

Sydney wasn't sure she liked the concerned expression in his eyes. Even after all they'd been through together, didn't he believe she could handle this?

"Sure thing—*James*," she snapped, suddenly annoyed with him.

Noah shrugged. "Just checking."

Sydney blew out a sigh of frustration. Why did she let him get to her?

Her hand wandered up to check her riding helmet, which was still on her head. She straightened it and fastened the safety strap. The modified riding crop was still in her pocket, and she pulled it out and handed it to Noah.

"Hang on to this for me, James," she said in her Tammy Rae voice. "I'll let you know if I need it."

Noah's eyes flashed dangerously at her, but he nodded and took the crop. "Of course, miss. Whatever you say."

They stood in silence for a minute or two. Sydney wished they could discuss how the mission was going so far—it might distract her from the coming ride—but there were too many people around to take that risk.

I thought I was finally getting over this kind of performance anxiety, Sydney thought. *I mean, all I have to do is ride a horse for a few minutes, not tame a wild elephant or something. After the last few missions I've been on, this kind of basic recon is practically a paid vacation.*

That made her feel a little bit better. She had faced down enemy agents and all sorts of other deadly dangers. The agency had prepared her for this mission as well. She would be fine.

She spotted Melanie coming toward them a moment later with Rocket in tow. The horse was tacked up in a jumping saddle and a rather complicated-looking bit and bridle.

"I'll hop on first so you can watch how she goes," Melanie offered. Leading the horse into the ring, she put her left foot in the stirrup and swung gracefully up into the saddle. "I'll just put her through some basics—let me know if you want to see anything in particular."

"Okay, thanks." Sydney watched as Melanie rode the mare around the ring. She wasn't quite sure what she was supposed to be looking at, but she was relieved to see that the horse seemed fairly calm under saddle. She went from walk to trot to canter and back again at Melanie's command, the mare's constantly moving ears the only hint of her alertness.

Noah leaned a little closer. "Don't forget, you're supposed to be making friends with this girl," he murmured into her ear, his warm breath tickling her skin. "We've got to get close to Lawton, and Melanie is our in."

"I know," Sydney said, her voice tight. "Don't worry. I'm on it."

Just then Melanie rode up to the fence and smiled at them. "Ready to give her a go?" she asked cheerfully.

Sydney gulped and nodded. "Ready as I'll ever be," she joked with a weak grin.

Melanie dismounted and glanced at Sydney's long legs. "I'd better let the irons down."

She fiddled with the stirrup leathers, then stepped back and nodded to Sydney. "Okay, that should suit you a little better. Want to hop on?"

"Sure." Taking a deep breath, Sydney stepped forward. She gave Rocket a quick pat on the shoulder. "Nice horse."

Rocket let out a snort and jumped away from her touch. "Stand!" Melanie chided the horse, moving her back into position. She glanced at Sydney. "Sorry about that. She's always a little antsy with new people."

"No problem." Sydney tried to sound as if she dealt with antsy horses all the time. Stepping forward again, she grabbed the back of the saddle with her right hand and lifted her left foot toward the stirrup. She managed to jam her toe in, but when she tried to bounce and swing herself up onto the horse's back as Melanie had done, her foot slipped, goosing the horse in the ribs. Rocket let out a loud snort and leaped away, and Sydney lost her balance and almost fell flat on her rear.

"Oops," she said with a sheepish laugh. "Guess my legs are still a little stiff from the long flight. Uh, is there a mounting block or something around here?"

"Afraid not. But no worries!" Melanie smiled at Noah. "James, you look like a strong chap. Could you give her a leg up? I'll hold Rocket's head so she doesn't move away again."

"Er, of course," Noah said, looking startled. "Glad to help."

Sydney wasn't sure Noah knew what he was supposed to do. On the pretense of bending over to adjust her boots, she leaned toward him as he approached. "Just grab my lower leg and hoist me up on the count of three," she whispered.

Noah nodded briefly. "Count of three, miss?" he said. "One . . . two . . . three!"

Sydney pushed off again. At the same time, she felt Noah's strong arms propel her up into the air. In fact, she had so much momentum this time that she nearly sailed right over the saddle and onto the ground on the other side.

Luckily Rocket held still, and Sydney managed to catch her balance and plant herself in the horse's saddle. She let out a sigh of relief and picked up the reins.

"Okay, y'all," she said. "Here we go!"

She nudged tentatively at the horse's sides with both heels, and Rocket immediately stepped into a fluid, rather fast walk. The mare's body was tense and quivering with barely suppressed energy, making Sydney feel as if she were straddling a keg of dynamite.

"Good girl," she murmured to the horse. "Easy, now. Easy."

She glanced around, glad to see that most of the other horses that had been in the ring when they'd arrived had finished and left. The only other rider remaining was at the far end of the ring and seemed to be staying there.

"She doesn't take much leg," Melanie called from over near the fence. "Just think it, and she'll do it. Want to try a trot?"

Before Sydney could answer, the mare flung up her head and broke into the faster gait. "Whoops!" Sydney cried breathlessly, automatically posting to the horse's rather choppy trot. "I think she heard you!"

"Don't worry, you're doing fine," Melanie

called. "She's a little hollow, but I can see that she's minding you pretty well. If you can stay relaxed yourself, she'll relax soon enough."

Part of Sydney's CIA training involved a focus on mind and body control. She had spent hours tensing and relaxing a single muscle on cue, or reciting words from a cue card despite various distractions such as extreme heat or cold, loud noises, or physical pain. The end result was a growing confidence in her own ability to withstand just about any physical challenge that came her way.

And that's what this is, after all, Sydney reminded herself as Rocket suddenly yanked her head forward, almost pulling her out of the saddle. *A physical challenge. That's something I know I can handle. And if Sloane and the others at HQ didn't think so too, they wouldn't have sent me on this mission.*

The thought alone seemed to give her an extra hint of control over the horse's movements. With a twitch of the reins and a nudge of her heels, she turned Rocket and started her trotting in the opposite direction. The mare flicked an ear at her and snorted but did as requested.

Just when Sydney was starting to enjoy herself, a rider entered the ring on a jittery-looking gray gelding. As the newcomer's helper started to close the metal gate behind the pair, the gray suddenly planted his feet and then backed up rapidly. The rider managed to get the horse moving forward again, but in the process the gray gelding kicked out. His shod rear hooves connected with the gate with a loud clang.

Rocket leaped sideways at the sudden sound, her ears flat back on her head. Sydney was thrown off balance, one of her feet coming out of its stirrup as the reins slid through her hands. She wasn't sure if the mare was in a true panic or just sensed an opening, but before Sydney could recover, the mare took off around the ring at a brisk canter that quickly turned into a gallop.

Clamping both legs against the horse's sides to hold herself in place, Sydney fished for her lost stirrup with one foot while doing her best to gather up the reins again. Rocket shook her head as she ran, the movement threatening to upset Sydney's balance once more as she felt her mount going faster and faster.

"Relax! Just go with her!"

Through her haze of panic, Sydney was vaguely aware of Melanie's words. Once again she called upon her training, forcing her body to respond to her mind's will. Her muscles relaxed slightly. As if by magic, the mare slowed down a little, her stride becoming smoother and more rhythmic. Before long Sydney was able to bring her down to a trot, and finally to an easy walk.

"Nicely ridden!" Melanie called out encouragingly. "I think she likes you."

Sydney let the reins slide through her fingers, breathing in and out and feeling quite pleased with herself for keeping her cool. *After this, trading punches with enemy agents will seem like nothing,* she thought with a slight smile.

As she rounded the corner at the end of the ring, she noticed a familiar bulky figure at the rail watching her ride. Immediately her whole body tensed up again, causing Rocket to toss her head and prance a few steps nervously. This time Sydney hardly noticed the mare's reaction. The man on the rail was Miles Lawton!

Trying not to let her excitement show, Sydney rode over to Melanie and Noah, halting Rocket near the fence. "That was interesting," Sydney said. "She's certainly very responsive. I'm sure I could learn quite a lot from a horse like this." While she was talking, she took one hand off the reins and pretended to adjust her helmet. Shooting Noah a meaningful look, she casually pointed one pinky finger toward Lawton.

Noah just as casually bent over as if to brush some dust from his pant leg. Sydney saw him glance toward Lawton.

Meeting Sydney's eye and nodding slightly, Noah stepped back from the fence. "If you won't be needing me, miss, I'll just go stretch my legs a bit," he said.

"Oh!" Melanie glanced at him. "Before you do that, James, would you mind running into the barn and asking my grooms to start getting Chipper ready for his warm-up? I just realized my ride time is getting close."

Anyone else would have missed the almost imperceptible grimace of annoyance that flashed across Noah's face. But Sydney was getting to know him very well.

"Of course, Miss Lawton," Noah said with a stiff half-bow. "I'll be happy to do that right away."

Sydney slumped in the saddle, disappointed, as he hurried off toward the barn without so much as a glance in Lawton's direction. What a time for Melanie to start treating Noah like the servant she thought he was!

Still, there wasn't much they could do about it.

It was more important to protect their cover than to tail Lawton again right at that moment. When she glanced toward Lawton again, she saw him turn away and disappear into the crowd.

Rocket shifted her weight uneasily under Sydney, her tail flicking from side to side. She lifted her head and snorted, seeming impatient with standing still.

Feeling as though she might be running out of luck in the riding department, Sydney quickly swung down from the horse and handed the reins to Melanie.

Melanie looked surprised. "Oh, are you finished already?" she asked, scratching the mare's white blaze. "Didn't you want to pop over a few jumps or something?"

"Not today, I don't think. Rocket is just darling. I think she and I could become very good friends," Sydney lied. "But I like to ride a new horse a couple of times and sort of think things over in between, you know?"

"Of course." Melanie stepped from one side of the mare to the other to run up her stirrups. "That makes perfect sense. Perhaps if you're planning to stay a few days, we can set up another ride for after the event? I stable my horses at home, and it's just a few clicks from here."

"That sounds perfect!" Sydney flashed Melanie her friendliest smile. "In the meantime, I'd love to know a little more about her when y'all have a chance. I'm sure you're very busy right now, getting ready to compete and all. Would you possibly have time to meet with me later and tell me a little more about her? Maybe we could get together for dinner or something?"

Melanie smiled. "That would be great. Why don't you join me for dinner this evening? If you don't mind coming out to my home, I could show you my other horses. I have a mare due to foal soon, and several youngsters I'm bringing along."

Sydney smiled. Clearly she hadn't overestimated Melanie's sense of Australian hospitality— or the eagerness of a horsewoman to discuss her favorite subject.

* * *

By the time Sydney and Noah reached their hotel suite a little while later, Sydney's legs felt like lead pipes welded stiffly to her body. Every step brought out new twinges of achiness.

"Ugh," she exclaimed, collapsing onto her back on the bed in her room. "And here thought I was in pretty good shape!"

Noah had followed her in. "Don't get too comfortable," he said. "We need to get changed and ready for dinner. But first we should talk about strategy."

Sydney rolled her head to the side to look at him, keeping the rest of her body perfectly still. Noah was standing just inside the doorway, staring down at her.

"What's to talk about?" she asked. "We're just looking for any signs of suspicious activity, right? I mean, we don't even know if Lawton himself is going to be there. I couldn't think of a way to ask earlier without sounding weird. Sounds like a play-it-by-ear kind of situation to me."

"Not exactly." Noah picked up Sydney's riding helmet, which she had dropped on a table on her way into the room. He turned it this way and that, staring at it intently. "I've been thinking about this all the way back here, and here's what we need to do. You're going to have to play decoy—keep Melanie occupied, and her father as well if he's there. Meanwhile, I'll slip away and do some snooping around. Shouldn't be too hard—rich people like that hardly notice the servants after a while."

He put a little extra emphasis on the word *ser-*

vant. Sydney stared at the ceiling, slightly amused. Noah was a man of action, and she guessed that he was frustrated by his limited role in the mission so far, even more so by having to play second fiddle to her, a young female rookie agent.

Still, that doesn't give him the right to start acting like a macho jerk and trying to take over, she thought.

"Listen," she began, pushing herself to an upright position on the bed. As she did, her thighs screamed with protest. Muscles she didn't even know she had started burning and spasming.

Sydney bit back a groan. Noah set down the riding helmet and looked at her sharply. "What?" he demanded. "You have a problem with the plan?"

Yes, Sydney thought. *The only plan I feel like making is for me to climb into a hot bath for about the next twelve hours.* Since that wasn't an option, she merely shrugged. "I guess not," she said calmly. The truth was, she hated the idea of playing such a passive role during their reconnaissance that evening.

But she also realized something important. *It's not worth picking a fight over,* she told herself. *Noah and I butt heads often enough as it is—better just to let this one go.*

Besides, the way her legs were aching at the moment, she figured that sitting in a nice dining room all evening sounded like just the ticket. "Okay," she said with a beatific smile. "I'll keep them distracted with my natural wit and charm while you play superspy. Sounds like a plan."

Noah looked surprised and a little suspicious at her reply. "Well, good," he said brusquely. "It's settled, then. I'm just going to shower and change clothes." He scowled. "I wish we didn't have to go there tonight in Lawton's hired car. Limits our options, big-time."

"Well, what was I supposed to say?" Sydney replied. "Melanie offered to send the car—I wasn't about to tell her 'No thanks, we'd rather drive ourselves so we can discuss your father, the scum-sucking terrorist supporter, in private. If you don't mind, of course.'"

"Very funny." Noah rolled his eyes and headed into his room.

Sydney collapsed back on the bed, relieved to have a few moments' rest. To distract herself from her aching muscles, she ran over the coming evening in her head. Now that her test ride on Melanie's horse was over, she could focus all of her attention on the mission. She wasn't really sure what they were supposed to be looking for, but she figured that was Noah's problem. Once they were inside Lawton's house, she just had to focus on her role as a distraction and give him the chance to look around. While she still wasn't thrilled with that role—it felt a little too close to playing it safe, letting her partner take all the risks—she was confident that she could do it well. That would have to be enough this time.

Realizing that Noah would be back for her soon, she rolled over and stood up, ignoring her protesting leg muscles. Peeling off her riding clothes, she popped a few aspirin and then quickly changed into a tailored pale peach silk pantsuit and strappy sandals and ran her fingers through her poufy blond wig. She glanced into the mirror over the dresser. She looked every inch the wealthy Texas belle. Sometimes it still amazed her how completely she was transformed by some of her disguises. Looking into a mirror could be like staring at a stranger. Noticing that her bright red lipstick had faded, she headed into the bathroom to fix it.

After touching up her makeup, she returned to the bedroom and opened her suitcase. Digging beneath the neat stacks of shirts and underwear, she pulled out a small duffel bag, unzipped it, and dumped its contents onto the bed. She stared at the array of items lying there, then grabbed a pair of gaudy gold earrings that hid tiny recording devices and put them on. She strapped on the leather camera belt from her earlier outfit and tucked a few other useful items into her handbag.

She might be just the decoy in that night's mission. But that didn't mean she wasn't going in prepared for anything.

5

"WOW. NICE PLACE," SYDNEY said, shooting Noah a meaningful look as their car pulled into the driveway of Lawton's estate, just a half-hour drive from the event grounds.

She knew it wasn't safe to say much else. Even though there was a glass window separating them from the uniformed driver up front, Sydney knew better than to trust that it guaranteed them any privacy.

She stared out the window, doing her best to memorize every detail of the castlelike home they were approaching. It was three stories of reddish stone and Tudor-inspired dark timbers, with numer-ous mullioned windows reflecting the rays of the setting sun. The paved drive swept around in a semicircle, flanked by hedges. A life-sized statue of a horse frolicked on a sweeping, grassy lawn. On one side of the house, another drive led back toward a cluster of buildings that Sydney guessed were the stables. In the broad, flat meadow on the other side of the house, three helicopters crouched like giant insects on a large, round launch pad. Several luxury cars were parked in a gravel area to one side of the main drive, along with a pair of expensive-looking horse trailers.

The car pulled smoothly to a stop in front of the broad wooden front doors. Melanie was standing on the front steps, and she hurried toward the car as the driver walked around to open the doors. Sydney gave her a little wave as she climbed out of the back-seat, doing her best to ignore her aching thighs.

"We're here," she announced in her best Tammy Rae twang.

"You're here! Welcome!"

Melanie seemed genuinely happy to see them, and Sydney felt a twinge of guilt. Was it really right to use such a nice person? What would Melanie think if she knew that her new "friend" Tammy Rae was only interested in spying on her father?

If he's anything like my father, maybe she wouldn't mind, Sydney thought ruefully. Shrugging off such distracting thoughts, she smiled at Melanie.

"Thanks," she said, gesturing to Noah, who was standing by the car. "Come along, James."

Melanie led them toward the front door. "I hope you don't have your heart set on any fancy tucker," she said apologetically. "We've all had such a busy day—I'm afraid I just got home thirty minutes ago, so the cook is scrambling to put something together."

"Never mind all that, I'm easy to please when it comes to food." Sydney laughed loudly. "So how did you do today? Your dressage test, I mean. I'm sorry we had to leave before you rode."

"That's all right." Melanie shrugged and smiled. "Dressage is a bit of a weak spot for me anyway—the fewer witnesses the better. But we did all right. Chipper and I wound up ninth in the standings after our test."

"That's great! Congrats," Sydney said, a little distracted by a sudden flash from somewhere above. She glanced up, wondering what had caused it. The estate's floodlights reflected off the upstairs windows, but nothing was moving that she could see.

"Thanks. We'll just have to see if Chipper and

I can manage not to come a gutser out on cross-country tomorrow!" Melanie laughed heartily. "Still, he's a great horse. I think we've got as fair a go as any."

Melanie reached for the handle of the front door, but before she could touch it the door swung open. A formally dressed butler was standing there. He bowed slightly and stood back to let them pass.

"Thanks, Bertram." Melanie gestured for Sydney to follow her inside. "Come on, I want you to meet Daddy. He's the one who's made it possible for me to own all these super horses."

"Great, I'd love to meet him," Sydney replied, following her hostess into the house.

She found herself in a spacious, wood-paneled foyer. A vaulted ceiling stretched three stories overhead, while a curving mahogany staircase led to stacked second- and third-floor balconies lined with modern artwork. Several arched doorways led off the foyer, and Sydney caught glimpses of luxurious furnishings, rich Oriental rugs, and other trappings of the very wealthy.

"Nice place y'all have here," she commented.

Melanie shrugged. "It's home, sweet home to me," she said. "Daddy loves this house—he designed it himself. He considers it his reward for his success in business."

"Oh?" Sydney was careful to maintain a casual, small-talk tone. "What line of business is he in?"

"Import/export," Melanie replied. "Very boring stuff—but don't tell him I said that."

As Sydney chuckled, she heard the sound of footsteps approaching from a hallway at the back of the foyer. A moment later Lawton appeared. He was still dressed in the dark suit from earlier that day, though his shoes had been replaced with leather mocs.

"Well, well," he said with a jovial smile that didn't touch his dark, wary eyes. "Who have we here?"

Melanie danced over to him, then took him by the arm and pulled him farther into the foyer. "This is my new friend Tammy Rae from America. She's the one I was telling you about earlier."

"Well, I'm happy to see that you're finally making some human friends instead of hanging out with those great hairy sooks of yours all the time," Lawton said with a slight upward twitch of his lip.

"Daddy!" Melanie tugged on his arm in playful protest. "Don't tease me in front of company."

"Sorry, sweetheart." This time Lawton's smile lit up his whole face, making him look for a moment like a completely different person. Sydney could plainly see that he adored his daughter.

Figures, Sydney thought, momentarily flashing to an image of her own father's dour, humorless face. *Even a suspected terrorist and all-around ruthless killer can manage to have a normal, loving relationship with his daughter. . . .*

Forcing that thought out of her mind, she extended her right hand. "It's so nice to meet you, Mr. Lawton. Thank you for having us over on such short notice."

Lawton's dark eyes were shrewd and suspicious as he took Sydney's hand. She did her best to keep her expression guileless as she smiled back at him. He squeezed her hand once, holding on to it for a long moment.

"A pleasure," he said at last, releasing her hand. "Any friend of my daughter's is always welcome here."

"You have a gorgeous home," Sydney said. "And an absolutely adorable daughter."

"Thank you. I'm very proud of both." Lawton waved toward an arched doorway behind him. "Won't you join me for a drink before dinner?"

"That sounds lovely." Sydney gestured to Noah, who was standing quietly by the door. "By the way, this is my personal assistant, James. I hope he won't be in the way—I do so hate traveling alone in a strange country. I thought perhaps he could help your people with the meal or something." She smiled beguilingly as Lawton stood back to usher her into a cozy, wood-paneled sitting room filled with hunting trophies and equestrian prints. "Back home in Texas, my mama taught me always to bring a little something when I'm invited to dinner—so I've brought James!"

Melanie chuckled. "It's quite all right, but I don't think we'll need to put him to work." She smiled at Noah, who had just followed them into the room. "Make yourself at home, James—you can consider it your night off!"

"Thank you, miss."

Sydney shot Noah a warning glance. She hadn't missed the slightly tight, strained tone in his voice.

Okay, maybe I'm taking the servant thing a little too far, she told herself. *Anyway, it's kind of nice to see that Noah is human after all—not Mr. Perfect Superspy who never lets anything bother him.*

Melanie walked over and hit a switch, and soft classical music drifted out of invisible speakers somewhere in the corners of the room. Even though it was quite warm outside, the inside of the house felt cool and slightly damp, and the crackling fire in the brick-lined fireplace added a cheery glow and warmth to the den.

"What a nice room," Sydney commented, trying not to shudder at the animal heads mounted on the walls—a cougar, several deer, and a startled-looking kangaroo. Aside from them, the place really was quite pleasant. She automatically noted that two other doors opened off of the room in addition to the one through which they'd entered. Working for SD-6 had quickly taught her always to look for escape routes.

As Sydney perched on the edge of a burgundy brocade sofa, a servant appeared with a tray of drinks. Near the fire, Lawton was settling himself into a distressed leather chair. "Saw you riding that mare of Mel's earlier, Ms. Fielding," he said abruptly. "She's a mean one."

For a second, a confused Sydney thought he was talking about Melanie. Then she realized he was referring to Rocket.

"Mean?" she said brightly. "Oh, I didn't find her mean at all. Matter of fact, I thought she was a real sweetie pie. Oh, and please—call me Tammy Rae."

"Don't be fooled," Lawton growled. "That mare is a bloody hard case. She's dangerous—I just about threw a party the day Mel decided to sell her. Crooked as that blaze of hers, that one."

Melanie laughed. "Some horse trader you are,

Daddy," she teased, though Sydney sensed an undercurrent of annoyance beneath her light tone. "How is poor Rocket ever going to find a nice new home if you keep talking her down?"

Lawton set his drink on a side table and stood, prowling restlessly toward the fireplace and back again. "You'll be lucky to give away that bodgy beast to the knackers, Melanie. Or maybe as a broodmare."

"Oh, rack off, Daddy," Melanie muttered. She cleared her throat. "In any case, I'm sure Tammy Rae can make up her own mind about Rocket."

Interesting, Sydney thought, noting the obvious tension that had sprung up between them. Did it indicate anything more than an ongoing father-daughter disagreement over a particular horse? She didn't know, but she added it to her mental list of observations.

Out of the corner of her eye, she saw Noah sidling toward the door. "Oh, Mr. Lawton," she purred, putting a hand on the man's arm and skillfully maneuvering him toward a nearby window. "Please tell me—who did that marvelous equestrian bronze outside there?" She pointed toward the statue on the lawn.

She listened with feigned fascination as Lawton described the artist's background and credits.

By the time the two of them turned away from the window, Noah had disappeared from the room. Sydney breathed a silent sigh of relief. That had been almost too easy.

"Well," she said, intending to keep the conversation going so the others didn't have time to notice her "servant's" absence. "What other sights would you suggest I see while I'm in—"

"Sir!" The butler they'd seen earlier appeared in the doorway, holding Noah by the elbow. The uniformed servant nodded briskly toward Sydney and Melanie. "So sorry to interrupt, ladies. But sir, I thought you would want to know that I just caught this fellow skulking around in the back hall."

Lawton narrowed his eyes. "Thank you, Bertram," he said. "You can leave him with us."

"I—I'm sorry, sir," Noah stammered as the butler loosened his grip and left the room. "I was just having a look and I guess I wandered a little too far off course."

If she hadn't known better, Sydney would have believed that Noah—or, rather, James—was truly abashed, confused, and a little frightened. She couldn't help being a little impressed with his acting skills. Was there anything he couldn't do?

"I'm sorry, too," Sydney apologized. "I don't know what gets into James sometimes—he just gets restless and has to stretch his legs. Don't you Aussies call that a walkabout?"

She laughed, and Melanie joined in. But the apologies didn't seem to satisfy Lawton. "How long have you employed this man?" he asked Sydney. "Did you check his background before hiring him? Where does he come from?"

"Daddy!" Melanie sounded embarrassed. "Please, don't start with your paranoia now. We're trying to have a nice evening. Who cares if James went for a little wander around the place?"

Lawton smiled briefly at his daughter. "Sorry, sweetheart," he said, his broad shoulders still tense and his fists clenched at his side. "But one can't be too careful these days. I'm sure a lady of Ms. Fielding's background can understand that."

"Of course," Sydney said quickly. "And don't worry, James will stay right here with us if you like." She knew that wouldn't exactly help them reach their goals. But the last thing she wanted to do was further arouse Lawton's suspicions.

Lawton was already shaking his head. "I have a better idea," he said. Walking over and pressing an intercom button near the door, he spoke into it. "Marcus, Phillips, get up here." He turned away from the intercom and stared at Noah, who was carefully keeping his head bowed and his eyes on the floor. "It might be best if James here spent the evening in the kitchen watching the telly with a couple of my boys. I'm sure you understand."

"Sure thing," Noah muttered. "Sorry to cause you any trouble, sir."

Sydney's heart sank as a pair of broad-shouldered servants appeared in the doorway—security guards, Sydney guessed, based on their muscles and the gun she could see peeking out from beneath the taller one's jacket. So much for Noah's spying plans! There was no way he was going to sneak away from the watchful eyes of those two—not unless he wanted to totally blow his cover. And no matter how impatient he was getting with his alias for the mission, he would never take that kind of chance.

Sydney realized what that meant. If they were going to find out anything important tonight, it was going to be up to her.

6

JUST A FEW MINUTES after servants had brought in the main course, Lawton glanced at his watch.

"Excuse me, ladies," he said abruptly, pushing back from the table and standing up. "It's later than I realized. I hope you'll excuse me—I have a meeting in town in a few minutes."

"Of course, Daddy," Melanie said, though she sounded disappointed.

Sydney smiled. "It was so nice meeting you, Mr. Lawton."

"Likewise. Enjoy the rest of your visit to Australia." He glanced at Melanie. "I've just got to dash upstairs and fetch a few things from my office. If my driver comes looking for me, tell him I'll only be a moment."

"Okay, Daddy," Melanie replied as Lawton walked around the table and gave her a quick kiss on the forehead. "Don't be too late, all right?"

"I'll try, sweetheart."

As Lawton hurried out of the room, Melanie sighed and poked at her roast beef with her fork. "Poor Daddy," she murmured. "He works so hard—sometimes I think it's the only thing he cares about."

Sydney shot her a sympathetic look. She could certainly relate to that. She could barely remember a time when her father hadn't spent practically every waking minute at his job. Even though she had all but cut him out of her life since starting college, it still made her feel lonely to think of all the dinners he'd missed or cut short because he had to go to a meeting or got an urgent call from the office.

But before she could speak, Melanie laughed and shrugged. "But then I realize I'm being silly to whinge about it. Daddy loves his work, but he also spends heaps of time and money on other things, like supporting local charities, and of course the eventing community. He's a real role model in this area to so many people. I'm really proud of him."

"Yes, I can see why," Sydney said politely. Secretly, though, she couldn't help feeling a little sorry for Melanie. How could she be so blind? Didn't she ever suspect that her father might not be what she thought he was? Hadn't she ever looked deeper?

"Anyhow, Daddy has always been supportive of my riding and such." She paused, staring down at her food. "That's why it's so difficult. . . . I'm sure you noticed that we had a bit of a blue back in the den—an argument, I mean—when we were talking about Rocket."

"Well, yes," Sydney admitted kindly. Meanwhile, all her senses went on alert as she remembered her earlier observation. "I did notice a bit of tension between y'all for a second there."

Melanie sighed. "It's because he wants me to sell Rocket to a friend of his, Mr. Rabik. He likes to buy up promising horses from here and over in New Zealand—he gets big bikkies for them overseas." She shrugged and bit her lip. "But I don't quite trust Mr. Rabik's horsemanship; it seems like too many of his horses never again live up to what they could do before he buys them."

"Oh, dear," Sydney commented in a sympathetic voice, hoping that Melanie would keep talking. She still wasn't sure that this had anything to do with their mission, but she was glad that she'd switched on the hidden recorders in her earrings when they'd sat down to dinner just in case.

"Besides, he wants Rocket as a broodmare off in Europe somewhere, and Daddy doesn't seem to understand that I'd rather see her keep competing while she's in her prime. She just loves it so much. . . ." Melanie glanced over at Sydney and laughed sheepishly. "Oh, can you believe me, yabbering away about my problems, when I might be able to solve them all by talking you into buying Rocket yourself." She grinned and winked at Sydney. "So what else do you want to know about her?"

For the next few minutes they chatted about Rocket, other horses, and riding in general. As usual, Sydney was grateful for the extensive personal profile and background information that SD-6 had provided her for the mission. She was able to reel off Tammy Rae's entire life story without hesitation, even though part of her wished she didn't have to continue with the charade. She still felt slightly guilty for deceiving such a genuinely nice person, for Melanie turned out to be just as funny and down-to-earth as her first impression had led Sydney to believe. Her easy laugh and optimistic outlook reminded Sydney a little bit of Francie—

like her roommate, Melanie Lawton was the type of person everyone liked right away; the type who always made others feel comfortable and happy. In a different life, Sydney was sure that she and Melanie could have been good friends.

They were chatting about favorite films over dessert and coffee when Melanie glanced at her watch. "I hope you won't think me a total yobbo, but I really ought to run down and check if my preggo mare's looking close to foaling yet. You could come along if you like—take a squizz at the barn and my other horses."

"That sounds great." Sydney realized that this could be her chance. With both Melanie and her father out of the house, she could take a quick look around—maybe find that upstairs office Lawton had mentioned earlier. "But first I need to excuse myself to the ladies' room."

"No drama," Melanie said cheerfully. "I'll wait for you."

Sydney shook her head quickly. "Oh, don't bother, darling," she said, faking an embarrassed laugh. "My family always says I take longer in the bathroom than Colonel Travis standing against the Mexican troops at the Alamo. Why don't I just meet you down there in a few minutes?"

"Well, all right," Melanie agreed. "Just head out any of the back doors and follow the lights." She gestured toward the rear of the house. "After I check on Misty, I really ought to do a few other things as well, so I'll be there a while. Just give a shout when you get there and I'll show you around."

"Sounds good." Sydney took one last bite of her dessert and then stood. "Thank you so much for dinner. It was delicious."

Melanie pointed her toward a powder room in a back hallway, and the two of them parted ways. Sydney strolled in the direction her hostess had indicated, but as soon as she heard a door shut behind Melanie, she spun on her heel and headed in the opposite direction.

As she followed her unerring sense of direction back to the front of the house, Sydney was on full alert. Even though Lawton and Melanie were out, she knew that there were still servants everywhere—at least half a dozen that she'd seen, along with who knew how many more in the kitchen and elsewhere. But at the moment, the hallway leading to the foyer was empty.

Soon Sydney was sprinting up the wide mahogany staircase. She stayed on her toes, glad for the thick carpeting that muffled her steps.

On the second floor, she stepped to the back of the balcony overlooking the front door and glanced down the hallways that led through the rest of the house. Then she looked up. She needed to find Lawton's office, but she had no idea where it was beyond "upstairs." Could that mean all the way upstairs on the third floor?

Better check there first, she decided quickly. *If Melanie comes back and catches me, it'll be a lot easier to explain being on the second floor than the third.*

The third-floor balcony looked exactly like the second except for the different paintings on the walls. Barely glancing at the artwork, Sydney chose a direction randomly and headed down the hall. She walked quickly but cautiously, listening for the slightest noise. The only light came from the plug-in safety lights that cast a faint yellow glow over the baseboards every twenty yards or so. All of the doors lining the hall were closed.

Sydney reached for the handle of the first door she came to, pausing just long enough to listen for movement inside. Easing the door open, she peered into the room. Moonlight pouring through the large windows showed it to be an ordinary-looking bedroom, the plastic cover over the spread indicating that it probably hadn't been used in some time.

Sydney reached down and snapped a photo with her belt camera, just in case.

Closing the door quietly behind her, she moved on. The next three doors also opened onto normal-looking bedrooms. Behind the one after that, she found a large, luxurious bathroom with an over-sized tub and a glass-enclosed shower stall.

Wondering if she was wasting her time on this floor, which seemed to serve as a guest wing, Sydney reached for the next handle, expecting to find more of the same. But this time the door didn't budge. It was locked.

Sydney's heart started pounding. She leaned against the door, pressing her ear to the wood and listening for any sound from within. A very faint, mechanical buzzing was barely audible over the slightly tinny sound of music.

Glad that she had come prepared, Sydney reached into the purse slung over her shoulder. From an interior pocket she pulled out what appeared to be a compact. When she flipped it open and peeled up the circle of beige face powder, she revealed a sophisticated lock-picking kit. She glanced at the doorknob, then selected one of the tiny tools. Thanks to her careful training, it was only a matter of seconds before she heard the lock click and felt it slide out of place. She slipped the compact back into her bag and then carefully eased open the door.

She almost gasped aloud as bright artificial light poured out through the crack in the door, nearly blinding her. Squinting against the glare, she peered in and saw a room about the same size as the bedrooms down the hall. But this room had nothing else in common with the others. The bright light came from half a dozen powerful fluorescent units overhead, which reflected off the high-gloss white walls and the shiny white tiles of the floor. Even the windows were covered in bright white shades. The furnishings were few and functional—a metal shelving unit along one wall, desks and worktables scattered here and there, a couple of metal chairs. But the room was hardly empty. Computers and computer parts were stacked everywhere—the tables, the shelves, the floor. Chips, wires, and switchboards spilled out of an open box, while floppy disks and stacks of paper littered the largest worktable in the center of the room.

At that table was a man. His back was to the door, and he was hunched over a keyboard, staring at a computer monitor in front of him. Sydney squinted at the monitor, trying to see what she could. Although the man's head blocked part of her view, she caught a glimpse of what seemed to be a blueprint of some kind of circuitry.

Then she noticed a distinctive swirl pattern on the man's balding head. Her eyes widened as she recognized the third man she'd seen at the stable with Lawton and the vet. Every instinct told her that this was what she and Noah were looking for—whatever was happening in this room, it was important to their mission. Fortunately, the sound of the music coming from the radio she'd heard earlier, as well as the buzz of the fluorescents, seemed to have covered the sounds of Sydney's breaking and entering, and the man remained totally focused on his work.

Keeping her gaze trained on the computer screen, hoping for a better look at the images on it, Sydney reached down for her belt camera and snapped several pictures of the room. She leaned forward, willing the man to tilt his head just a few inches to one side or the other. Maybe then she could get a clear shot of that computer. Or maybe if she leaned just a little farther into the room . . .

As she twisted to one side, trying to see the screen, her elbow hit the edge of the door. Sparks of pain flew through her arm as the impact sent the door flying all the way open with a thunk.

The man jumped and spun around in his chair at the noise. Sydney barely caught a glimpse of his surprised face as her instinct and training took over and she ducked back out of sight into the darkened hall.

"Hey!" the man shouted, heavy footsteps racing across the tile. "Who's out there?"

7

HEART POUNDING AND ADRENALINE pumping, Sydney sprinted down the hallway. She didn't know whether the man had gotten a look at her or not. If he hadn't, she wasn't about to give him a second chance.

Reaching the balcony, she grabbed the railing and vaulted over, swinging herself back in and onto the second-floor balcony below. Landing on the balls of her feet, her bent knees and ankles absorbing most of the shock, she quickly sprang up and took off down the closest hallway. She could hear the sound of running footsteps overhead—and after a moment, she was pretty sure she heard more than one set. She guessed that the man had sounded some kind of alarm.

Lights came on overhead, shouts came from the floor below, and Sydney knew she had to get out of sight pronto. She figured her best hope was to find a bathroom on the second floor, get inside, and play dumb.

That's if that guy didn't actually get a look at me, she thought with a brief stab of panic. *If he did . . .*

Pushing that thought aside, she started opening doors. The first two rooms were bedrooms, and she moved on quickly, expecting to find a third bedroom next in line, just as she had upstairs.

When she opened the third door, she gasped in surprise. The room inside was white-painted and tiled like the computer lab upstairs. But instead of shelves and switchboards, this room was lined with over a dozen large dog crates. Inside every one of them was a large German shepherd or rottweiler. Sydney sucked in her breath as the dogs all turned and stared at her alertly, their ears pricked up and their eyes glistening. But none of them let out even a single bark.

Their silence allowed Sydney to hear the ominous *click-click-click* of toenails on the tile. Glancing in the direction of the sound, she saw a very large, very healthy-looking German shepherd walking out from behind one of the occupied crates. The dog wore a collar but was otherwise completely unrestrained.

Sydney gulped. "Goo-oo-ood puppy," she cooed, backing away slowly. "Ni-i-i-ice little doggy-woggy . . ."

At the sound of her voice, the dog bounded toward her, its long pink tongue lolling out from between its sharp, glistening white canines. A silvery thread of drool trailed back from its jaws and stuck on the glossy dark fur around its ruff. As the dog came at her, Sydney jumped back and slammed the door shut, hoping that the latch would hold the creature back. But the dog body-slammed the door, sending it flying open again. It leaped into the hall and skidded to a stop facing Sydney.

Sydney automatically adapted a fighting stance, her hands trembling slightly as she raised them in front of her. She'd practiced fending off large guard dogs in her training, but she hadn't faced one yet in real life. She only hoped she remembered what to do. . . .

The dog jumped toward her. Sydney raised her

arms, but it was no good. The dog's weight sent her reeling, her back and shoulder smacking into the wall behind her and momentarily stunning her.

As Sydney desperately tried to shake off her wooziness and fight off her attacker, she was vaguely aware that she was not, in fact, being mauled. Instead, the dog stood on its hind legs, its paws on her shoulders, and eagerly licked her face, leaving her with dog slobber from forehead to chin. After a moment it let out a single bark, turned away, and ran down the hall toward the stairs with its tail wagging happily.

Sydney blinked in surprise, then quickly regained her senses as she realized that the loose dog might be just the sort of distraction she needed. Turning in the opposite direction, she continued her search for a bathroom.

She yanked open the next door in the row and stopped short, staring inside. "Jackpot!" she murmured.

In front of her was what had to be Lawton's office. The room was dominated by a huge oak desk with a computer at one end and a pair of telephones at the other. Several bookshelves behind the desk were filled to overflowing with books, magazines, and other paperwork, much of it tucked into file folders. Piles of papers were stacked neatly over most of the surface of the desk, and more papers overflowed onto the pair of guest chairs in front of the desk as well as the floor nearby.

Sydney slipped into the room and pulled the door shut behind her. Somewhere in the distance she heard the sounds of shouts and barking, but she ignored it. She wouldn't have much time, and she wanted to find out as much as possible while she was here.

Moving quickly across the floor to the desk, Sydney scanned its surface. Near the computer she noticed a framed photo of Melanie standing beside a tall gray horse, and another that had to be her as a child aboard a stout spotted pony. Once again Sydney couldn't help marveling at the relationship between the ruthless criminal and his sweet, unsuspecting daughter.

But there was no time to waste on such thoughts. Eschewing her belt camera, which seemed too awkward to use in this situation, she dug into her purse and quickly located the tiny camera Graham had built into an ordinary-looking key ring. She rotated slowly on one heel, snapping pictures of everything on the desk. Then she sat down in the leather desk chair and began going through the piles of papers, though she couldn't figure out much of what she was looking at.

Most of the paperwork seemed to have to do

with horses. There were pedigree charts, breeding contracts, registration papers, shipping and quarantine reports, and more. One pile held nothing but copies of newspaper clippings about horse shows and events, many of them featuring Melanie but others involving people and horses that were completely unfamiliar.

Sydney snapped a few more photos, but she was starting to wonder if any of what she was seeing would matter to SD-6. Maybe this office was nothing more than a place to organize his daughter's horse business. Surely he wouldn't keep records of his criminal activities right here in his home—that would be the first place the authorities or his enemies might look. Sydney felt a churning in the pit of her stomach. Had she just blown her cover for nothing?

As she was shuffling through a stack of quarantine reports, she suddenly stopped short and stared at a particular sheet. Most of the addresses of the reports were in London or Paris or Berlin, but this one was in Malaysia. Shifting through the rest of the pile more carefully, she spotted several more Malaysian addresses as well as some from Eastern European countries.

Interesting, Sydney thought, snapping pictures of the addresses.

But she had no idea if they actually meant anything. Despite her premission cram session, she still didn't really know much about the horse business—for all she knew, horses might be exported from Australia to Malaysia or Croatia all the time. For a second she wished Noah were there. He always seemed to know what meant something and what was just a dead end.

But he's not here, Sydney told herself firmly. *That means it's up to me to gather whatever information I can. The people back at HQ can sort out what it all might mean.*

Suddenly she became aware that the faint shouts and footsteps that she'd been hearing for the past few minutes were getting much louder. Glancing up sharply, she realized that it was probably only a matter of seconds before someone opened the office door.

"Well, find her!" a voice shouted from somewhere very close by.

Sydney gulped. Even muffled by the door, Lawton's voice was unmistakable. Apparently he had returned from his meeting.

"Uh-oh," Sydney whispered, looking around frantically. Judging by the sounds, it was too late to duck back out into the hall. She glanced briefly at the office window, already estimating the distance to the ground below. But the sight of the solid security bars on the window put an immediate end to such thoughts.

There was a second door in the room, this one behind the desk on one side of the bookshelves. Sydney had noted it upon entering, but she had no idea if it led to another room or merely into a closet. Either way, she decided it might be her only chance.

The heavy footsteps in the hall came to a stop right outside the office door. As the doorknob started to turn, Sydney silently pulled open the second door and glided through it.

8

INSTEAD OF THE CRAMPED closet she had expected, Sydney found herself in another room. The moonlight coming through the window glinted on stainless steel fixtures and a large vanity mirror, and Sydney realized that it was a bathroom.

Now I find it! she thought ruefully. She could already hear several loud voices in the office behind her. More voices rang out from somewhere behind the second door in the little room, which she assumed led into the hall. How many people were looking for her, anyway? And what would they do when they found her?

Staring at her pale, panicky-looking reflection in the mirror, she saw the rhinestones set into her fingernails sparkling in the moonlight. She glanced down quickly at her left thumb. Should she use her signaling device to call Noah?

No, she realized almost immediately. *He won't have time to find me before Lawton and his men do, and even if he could, we'd both still have to get past them. All this signal would do is give us away for sure. No, there must be another way out of this. . . .*

Glancing at the bathroom's two small windows, she noted with dismay that they, too, were blocked by security bars. She didn't seem to have much choice. She was going to have to talk—or fight—her way past Lawton.

Darting over to the second door, she flipped on the light switch beside it. As the glow of the dozens of round lightbulbs set around the vanity mirror illuminated the small room, Sydney yanked her purse from her shoulder and quickly dumped its contents onto the counter by the sink. The voices in the other room seemed to be moving toward the bathroom door. She didn't have much time.

Sydney scrabbled through the pile of cosmetics and other items on the counter. The first thing her hand closed around was a lipstick case. Planning to play dumb and pretend she'd been primping this whole time, she flipped off the top of the case as she was raising it to her lips—and wound up almost blinded by the powerful search beam that shot out from inside.

Rats! Sydney thought, flustered. *I forgot. And after Graham spent about half an hour showing me how this works, too. . . . Good thing I didn't pull this out at dinner, or Lawton really would've had a reason to be suspicious!*

Irritated with her own carelessness, she tried to recap the lipstick, but the top slipped out of her hand and clattered to the floor. Dropping to her hands and knees, she fished under the sink for it. But the cap seemed to have disappeared. Leaping over toward the toilet, Sydney lifted the lid and flicked the lipstick searchlight inside. But when she closed the toilet lid, she could still see bright yellow light shining out from inside. With a grimace, she quickly fished the lipstick case from the water, wiped it on her pant leg, and stared at it. As she turned back toward the counter, wondering if her purse lining would hide most of the light, she felt her foot hit something small and light. Diving to the floor again, she retrieved the lipstick top and quickly closed it over the searchlight.

The voices in the other room were moving closer to the door. Taking a deep breath, Sydney dropped the lipstick onto the pile on the counter and picked up a small bottle of lavender-scented hairspray. She spritzed the air with it, hoping to make it smell as if she'd been in there for some time. Then she grabbed a comb.

She was carefully teasing a few strands of her blond wig in the mirror when Lawton burst into the room a split-second later. "She's in here!" he shouted, his angry words echoing in the small room.

"Oh!" Sydney shrieked in pretend surprise, dropping the comb and spinning around to face him with her hand clutched to her heart. "Oh, my! You startled me!"

Melanie was pushing past her father, looking annoyed. "See, Daddy?" she cried. "You're going crazy for no reason! I told you Tammy Rae was in the ladies' room!"

Lawton didn't take his eyes off Sydney as he answered his daughter. "You told me she was in the powder room downstairs."

Sydney gave an apologetic little laugh. "Oh, that's where she sent me, Mr. Lawton," she said. "But I'm afraid that tiny little mirror there just wasn't up to the task of dealing with my hair." She put a hand to her poufy blond wig. "See, we like everything big back in Texas, hairdos included. I just couldn't get a full view of things down there, so I went and found myself a bigger bathroom." She gave him what she hoped was a convincingly charming smile. "I didn't think you'd mind, y'all have been so hospitable and all."

"Of course we don't mind," Melanie answered quickly, glaring at Lawton. "Don't pay any attention to my father—he's gone insane."

Lawton scowled. "It's not insane to worry about strangers wandering through my house," he snapped.

"Daddy!" Melanie shouted back, her hazel eyes flashing. "Just quit it, will you? I know you want me to sell Rocket to your friend. But that doesn't mean you have to try to scare away any other buyers I find, or accuse an innocent visitor of some crazy lurk! That's just not bloody fair!"

Lawton blinked and took a step back in the face of his daughter's fury. "Look, that's not why . . . ," he began.

"Stuff it, Daddy," Melanie said sharply. She turned to Sydney. "So sorry about that, Tammy Rae," she said in a softer voice. "I do hope you'll forgive my father. As I said earlier, he's a bit paranoid." She shot Lawton a glare. "It's not his best quality."

"Oh, no problem," Sydney said with a cheery

Tammy Rae smile. "I'm just so sorry to have caused such a ruckus. I certainly didn't mean to."

Lawton grumbled a few words that Sydney supposed were meant to be an acceptance of her apology. Then he quickly excused himself and hurried out of the bathroom—but not before shooting Sydney one last suspicious glare. Sydney gulped. Lawton might be backing down, but that didn't necessarily mean her excuses had convinced him.

Melanie didn't seem to notice anything. "It's not at all your fault." She sighed. "One of Daddy's dogs got out of its room, and apparently it ran around causing quite a fuss opening doors and startling people. That's got him all worked up."

Sydney started piling her things back into her purse. "Well, I suppose that's only natural."

"No, it's really not." Melanie stared at herself in the mirror, her expression uncharacteristically somber. "I worry about Daddy sometimes. He gets so wrapped up in his business, so stressed. It can't be healthy for him."

Sydney winced slightly on her new friend's behalf. It was becoming more obvious than ever that Melanie really had no idea that her father was leading a double life.

Still, how could she know? Sydney thought. *I'm sure a man like Lawton has learned to cover his tracks pretty well over the years. He'd have to, if even half the stuff SD-6 suspects about him is true. Besides, he so obviously adores Melanie. He wants to protect her, and keep her thinking they're just an ordinary family. Didn't he prove that just now? I'm sure he would've liked nothing more than to drag me off somewhere and have those guard dogs of his chew me into confessing what I was really up to, but he still wasn't willing to break cover in front of his daughter.*

"Well, anyway, I'm sorry to have upset him." Sydney dropped the last few items into her purse and snapped it shut. "But it's getting late, and you have a big day tomorrow. I suppose I'd better be going now."

Melanie looked upset. "Oh, please tell me you won't hold my grumpy old father against me or Rocket," she begged. "I do hope you'll still come out to see the cross-country tomorrow."

"Bless your heart!" Sydney exclaimed with a chuckle. "Of course I won't hold it against y'all. And I wouldn't miss cheering you on tomorrow for the world."

"Ace!" Melanie looked relieved. "You're so sweet, Tammy Rae. I know Rocket would be lucky to get a new owner like you."

Sydney smiled. "Thanks, honey," she said. "Now, where should I collect James?"

* * *

An hour later Sydney and Noah were walking across the darkened event grounds. The place was nearly deserted—just a few night lights burned in the temporary barns, and the distant sound of a tractor indicated that someone was still cleaning up from the day's activities.

Sydney had just finished filling Noah in on her adventures. She'd left out a few minor details—like being slimed by the not-so-vicious guard dog, and accidentally setting off the lipstick search beam. But she carefully described everything she'd seen in the computer room and Lawton's office, trying not to leave out a single thing.

Noah shook his head when she finished up the story with Lawton's reaction to finding her in the bathroom. "And where am I this whole time?" he grumbled. "Down in the smelly kitchen watching some incomprehensible Australian soap opera on TV." He grimaced. "What a waste—with both of us looking around, we probably could have really found out something."

Sydney wrinkled her nose in the dark. But she decided not to take offense at the comment. "Well, I'm totally convinced that Lawton is up to no good," she said. "I just have no idea what exactly he's doing. All the paperwork in that office seemed to be about horses."

"I thought there would have been something," Noah muttered, his brows pinched in the way that showed he was thinking hard. "He's probably keeping anything that might be incriminating out of his home."

Sydney nodded, not bothering to mention that she'd already come to the same conclusion. It had been a very long day, following a very long plane ride to get there, and a creeping sense of exhaustion was finally beginning to overtake her. "So when are you going to tell me what we're doing here now?"

"I want to check out that barn where you saw Lawton earlier," Noah replied, walking a little faster toward the stabling area. "If you're sure that man you saw in the computer room is the same one he was meeting with here . . ."

"I'm positive." Sydney had almost forgotten about the computer room and the man inside. She wasn't sure why Noah had suddenly decided it was important to investigate the site of that barn meeting she'd witnessed, which seemed to have been horse business rather than terrorist-supporting business. But she figured it was as good a starting point as any, especially considering the connection with the man in the computer room. At the very least, maybe a look around would help them figure out his identity and his connection with Lawton.

The two of them strode on in silence for a few minutes. Sydney's arms and legs felt like they had lead weights attached to them, but she was careful not to lag behind. If Noah was ready to keep going, so was she.

When they reached the row of wooden barns, Sydney pointed to the one she'd entered earlier. "That's the place," she said. "They went through that doorway and stood in front of the third stall on the left."

"Okay. Let's go. But be careful—just in case."

They walked silently to the doorway and peered inside. Sydney held her breath, listening for any hint of human activity within. But the only sound was the soft, rhythmic chewing of horses.

"I think it's clear," Noah whispered, creeping forward through the entrance.

The two of them carefully made their way to the stall in question. Sydney peered inside and saw a bay gelding munching at the pile of hay in the back corner. Was it the same horse the men had been discussing? She wasn't sure.

"Hey, boy," she said softly, lifting her hand to the animal's soft nose as it wandered over to the door to snuffle at them curiously.

Noah shot her a glance. "Come on," he said. "This is no time to play My Little Pony."

Rolling her eyes, Sydney tossed him a mock salute. "Aye-aye, Captain," she said. "I almost forgot—with you, it's all business all the time."

Noah glared at her. She glared back. There was a long moment of silence.

"Let's get to work," Noah muttered at last.

Without another word, they moved away from each other. Sydney carefully opened the stall door and stepped inside, talking softly to the horse. The animal gazed at her curiously for a moment before returning to his hay. Sydney quickly examined the interior of the stall for anything unusual. She peered into the water bucket, kicked at the bedding to see if there was anything hidden there, even pulled the salt block out of its holder on the wall and shook it.

But nothing seemed out of place, and so she exited the stall. Outside, she started examining every inch of the barn aisle. Noah was a little farther down doing the same thing.

"What are we looking for, anyway?" Sydney asked after a few minutes.

Noah shrugged. "Not sure," he said. "Just anything that might mean something."

"Well, that clears that up," Sydney muttered.

"Ha, ha, very funny," Noah replied with a hint of a smile. He walked toward her. "Seriously, I'm not really sure. But I'm really starting to wonder if we should be paying more attention to all this horse business instead of just assuming it's a cover or whatever. I mean, judging from what you found in his office, Lawton is really involved in this stuff— horse trading, exporting, the whole nine yards. Why would a man like him be so into something like that? It seems pretty far-fetched to call it mere fatherly interest."

Sydney shrugged. "He *does* seem to be a pretty interested father, though," she pointed out. "I mean, he and Melanie are really attached to each other. It's kind of sweet."

Noah let out a snort. "Yeah," he muttered. "That's the first word I'd think of to describe Miles Lawton—sweet."

"You know what I mean." Sydney frowned at him. "Anyway, what possible connection could there be between high-level event horses and international terrorism? It just doesn't make sense. It's not like you hear of a lot of suicide bombers riding in on Thoroughbreds."

"I don't know." Noah knitted his brow. "All I know is that we're still basically clueless, Lawton's up to dangerous business, and we've pretty much blown our cover. I'm starting to wonder if we should pull out."

Sydney bit her lip, recognizing the implications of his comment. If their cover was blown, it was her fault—she was the one who had blown it by not being more careful.

They worked in silence for a moment before Sydney spoke again. "Okay, so maybe Lawton is suspicious of us," she said. "But he still doesn't know anything for sure. It would be a shame to leave just when we might be getting somewhere."

"But Sloane specifically told us not to take any unnecessary risks," Noah argued. "This mission is supposed to be strictly intel gathering."

"Well, we could at least stick around for tomorrow's competition." Sydney waved one hand toward the quiet grounds outside the barn. "I mean, this event is going to be a crowded public affair. Lawton isn't likely to try anything here, no matter how suspicious he might be."

"Are you willing to bet your life on that?" Noah asked grimly.

Sydney shrugged and leaned on the stall door. "Don't be so dramatic," she told him tartly. "Anyway, if we do run into him here tomorrow, at the very least we should be able to get a pretty good idea whether he's on to us," she added with all the logic her exhausted brain could muster. "If he is, then we make a plan from there. But if he's not, it would be silly to pull out now, just when I'm getting tight with Melanie."

"I suppose that almost makes sense," Noah said grudgingly. He leaned on the door beside her, so close that Sydney could smell the lingering scent of his aftershave. With a loud sigh that startled the horse inside the stall, making it prick up its ears at him and snort, Noah glanced at her somberly. "All right. We'll try it your way."

9

WHEN SYDNEY AND NOAH arrived at the event grounds the next day, the air was electric. It was cross-country day—the central and defining portion of the three-day event, when competitors would gallop over a long, winding course jumping huge, solid obstacles built out of logs, stone, and other natural materials. Hundreds of spectators had turned out to enjoy the day's sport. People were setting up picnic blankets and tailgate parties, while children played games of tag or kickball on the wide swaths of grassy lawn that lay between the lanes of the course. The food vendors' business was already booming, the odors of hot buttered popcorn and grilling meat drifting along on the slight breeze. Talk and laughter filled the air, and there were dogs everywhere.

Once again Sydney was dressed in full equestrian regalia, though she couldn't help feeling slightly foolish about it. "It's not like I'm going to be riding today," she muttered to Noah. "I told you I should have worn normal clothes—might help me blend in."

Noah raised one eyebrow at her. "Does Tammy Rae really want to blend in?" he asked innocently. "If she did, I don't think she'd be wearing that exact shade of fire-engine red lipstick, now, would she?"

Sydney gritted her teeth, knowing that this was his way of getting back at her for all the servant jabs. Besides, maybe he was right. Tammy Rae wasn't the type to blend into the woodwork. Still, Sydney couldn't quite bring herself to wear her velvet riding helmet, carrying it tucked under one arm instead.

Before long she was enjoying herself too much to worry about what she was wearing. Even though she and Noah had found nothing the night before at the barn, they still intended to keep a lookout for Lawton or either of his mystery associates.

As she wandered through the crowds, enjoying

the festival atmosphere, Sydney was only about half on alert. She really wasn't expecting much to happen at the event that might be of interest to their mission. If Lawton showed up at all, she suspected it would only be to watch his daughter ride.

"When is Melanie supposed to go?" Noah asked, checking his watch.

"Soon." Sydney glanced at her watch. "Her scheduled start time is in about ten minutes, and they seem to be running on time. Do you want to watch her take off from the start box, or just find an interesting jump and cheer her over it?"

"Whatever." Noah looked less than interested in the choice. He scanned the crowds nearby. "We probably ought to keep moving around, though. We don't want to miss anything by staying too long in one spot."

Sydney shaded her eyes with one hand against the hot Australian sun, trying to see the number on the jump at the bottom of the next hill. "I heard some girls talking about jump twelve," she said. "It's supposed to be one of the toughest on the whole course. I see eleven down there—why don't we try to find twelve and watch for Melanie there?"

Noah shrugged, which Sydney took as an assent. She hurried down the hill with him following. Soon they were wandering past what appeared to be an impromptu Hacky Sack tournament on the fringe of the crowd surrounding jump twelve. Sydney peered over the heads of the people along the rope course marker and saw that the notorious number twelve was the type of obstacle known as a coffin—two solid jumps on either end of a sharp decline, with a ditch at the bottom. Horse and rider had to jump over the first fence, take a stride downhill, and leap over the ditch, then fit in an uphill stride while maintaining enough momentum to make it over the second jump.

As Sydney watched, a horse and rider approached the jump. The horse pricked up its ears alertly at the first jump. The rider adjusted his position, slowing the horse slightly, and the pair jumped in easily. The horse scrambled slightly getting over the ditch, losing a bit of momentum, and its hind hooves smacked loudly on the second jump. But the pair made it over, and the rider urged the horse back into a gallop as they headed down a long, fairly steep hill on their way to the next jump, which was located somewhere ahead in a patch of woods.

Sydney realized her heart was pumping just watching. "Wow, and they say *our* job is dangerous," she commented to Noah.

He shot her a warning glance. "What was that, miss?"

Oops. Sydney realized that she'd forgotten for a moment that she was supposed to be playing a role. That didn't happen much anymore—she was getting used to living a double life. But on the rare occasions when she did slip, it embarrassed her more than ever.

"I suppose dear Melanie will be along soon," she said loudly in her Tammy Rae voice. "She's riding a horse named Chipper today, James. I don't know if that's his show name or just his barn name, though."

Noah looked slightly confused. "What happened to that horse you rode yesterday? Why isn't Melanie riding her today?"

Sydney couldn't help feeling slightly smug for knowing something Noah didn't. "Didn't you read that packet they gave us before we left? If Melanie were riding Rocket in this event, she couldn't have let me ride her," she said. "There's a rule about that—only the competitor can ride the horse during the event, even off hours."

"Oh." Noah looked only mildly interested.

He turned to scan the crowd again. Sydney was about to jokingly ask him if he was trying to make his head swivel all the way around like an owl when he grabbed her by the elbow.

"Check it out," he said without moving his

lips. His voice was tense and excited. "Lawton. He's here. And it looks like he's not happy about something."

Sydney immediately snapped back into full spy mode, mentally kicking herself for letting her guard down. This was a mission, not a vacation—she shouldn't have forgotten that. If Noah hadn't been paying attention, she never would have noticed that Lawton was nearby.

Following Noah's gaze, she peered through the shifting crowds. Finally she spotted Lawton's familiar bulky form. He appeared to be arguing with his companion, a familiar-looking balding, ruddy, moonfaced man.

"That's the guy," she whispered excitedly to Noah. "The one I saw in the barn and in the computer lab!"

"Let's try to get closer," Noah murmured. "We don't want to let Lawton see us, though."

Sydney nodded and followed as Noah wound his way through the ever-shifting crowd. Soon they were only a few yards from the two men. They ducked behind a large generator powering several nearby food booths, which hid them from view. Unfortunately, the steady *chug-chug-chug* of the generator also drowned out the sounds of the men's voices.

"Let's see if we can—" Noah began.

The sound of the PA system drowned out his next words. "Now on course," the announcer's voice crackled out of the nearest speaker, which happened to be almost directly overhead, "we have Melanie Lawton on Chipper."

At the sound of his daughter's name, Lawton suddenly glanced toward the course. He then turned back to his companion and poked him sharply in the chest, muttering something Sydney couldn't hear. The second man nodded curtly in response, his lips set into a grim frown.

"Looks like they're finishing up their little meeting," Noah murmured.

Sure enough, Lawton scowled at the second man one last time, then spun on his heel and marched up the hill in the direction of the first section of the course. In the meantime, the second man hurried off the opposite way, heading toward a cluster of trees just beyond jump twelve.

"You follow that guy," Noah hissed, nodding after the stranger. "I'll take Lawton. He's less likely to notice me tailing him than Tammy Rae."

Sydney nodded, immediately realizing that he was right. She couldn't help feeling a twinge of disappointment. Melanie would be galloping past jump twelve in just a few minutes. And now it looked as though Tammy Rae wouldn't be there to cheer her on as she'd promised.

Oh, well, Sydney thought, trying not to flash to the many images of Francie's disappointed face in similar circumstances. *Duty calls. . . .*

Not sparing a backward glance for Noah, who was already melting into the crowd, she hurried after the stranger. He was walking briskly, his hands in the pockets of the windbreaker he was wearing despite the warm weather, looking neither right nor left as he made his way toward the patch of woods. The course entered the woods in a relatively open, airy section of tall trees, but the man ducked into some thick underbrush a few dozen yards to the left of that area.

There weren't many spectators in this section of the course. Sydney guessed that few people wanted to make that long trek back up the hill. That meant her job was going to be a little harder, since she wouldn't have much cover. She stuck closely to the course, trying not to look like she was hurrying. She followed the footpath that entered the woods beside the course ropes, listening carefully for sounds of activity to the left. Remembering her modified riding helmet, she put it on and flipped the switch to activate the receiver.

Almost immediately, she heard the murmuring

of multiple voices from some distance ahead. Stopping to listen, she realized she had to be listening to the voices of the few hardy spectators who had hiked down to the next jump. Based on the volume, she estimated that they were fifty or more yards ahead through the woods. She peered in that direction, but the course twisted and turned and she couldn't see any sign of jump or spectators through the thick forest.

Then her helmet picked up the sound of a low, muttered oath from somewhere much closer. She jumped back into the woods, her senses on high alert. Crouching down in a cluster of leafy bushes, she forced herself to wait and listen.

A moment later she caught a glimpse of motion out of the corner of her eye. Turning her head in that direction, she crouched even lower and then stayed perfectly still as her quarry slipped out of the cover of the trees and glanced up and down the course.

Sydney held her breath. What was the man doing?

He checked his watch, then looked up the course again. Sydney held her breath.

The man darted out onto the course, ducking under the rope that marked the boundary. He jogged straight across, then ducked under the rope on the other side. Crouching in front of a tree, he fumbled in his jacket pockets.

Sydney leaned forward, squinting in the dappled light filtering through the treetops. What in the world was he doing? For a moment she wondered if she was about to witness something that the man should have been doing in the privacy of a Porta Potti. Then she saw him straighten up and back away from the tree. His hands were in front of him, and for a moment Sydney still had no idea what was happening.

He ducked under the first rope and backed across the course, moving carefully but quickly. As he got closer, Sydney finally was able to see that his hands were unreeling a roll of thin, almost invisible wire, the end of which he had apparently just tied around that tree about a foot and a half above the ground. He was stretching the wire right across the course! As she watched in horror, he ducked beneath the rope on her side of the course, turned, and started to loop the wire around another tree.

Sydney's mind was already flashing through the terrible images of what would happen if a horse galloped into that wire without seeing it. The man finished tying off the second end of the wire, then pulled out a small pair of snips and cut it off. He glanced back out at the trip wire across the course, seeming satisfied with his work.

At that moment, the faint sound of the PA announcer's voice drifted toward her from some unseen, distant speaker. *"Still on course is Melanie Lawton,"* it said. *"She's just made it safely over the coffin at twelve, and is coming down and into the woods. . . ."*

Sydney didn't stop to think. Leaping forward impulsively, she ran toward the course and started waving her arms just as a rider on a big gray horse galloped into view around the corner at the end of the lane.

"Stop!" she cried. "You have to stop!"

She ducked under the rope, still waving her arms. She barely had time to register the startled look on Melanie's face when the horse let out a startled scream and leaped to one side, tossing his head.

"Whoa!" Melanie yelled, trying to hold on to her flying reins. "Chipper, quit it!"

Sydney gasped as the horse skidded back in the other direction, almost going down. As the gray gelding recovered his balance and threw in a buck, Sydney suddenly noticed movement out of the corner of her eye. She spun around and saw the man in the windbreaker sprinting toward her, an expression of twisted fury on his round face.

As she jumped aside to avoid his attack, Sydney heard Melanie gasp. "Tammy Rae? And Rabik!" she cried. "What are you guys doing—"

A sickening thud cut off the rest of her question. Spinning around, Sydney saw that Chipper had torn through the boundary ropes and crashed hard against a large tree at the side of the course. Melanie flew out of the saddle in the opposite direction, hit a second tree, and slumped to the ground. Chipper reared and then skittered back through the rope onto the course, where he started bucking again and again.

"Melanie!" Sydney cried. She leaped toward her.

Suddenly her mind exploded in a fiery torrent of pain. Her hands flew to her throat as razor-thin wire tightened around it, digging into her skin.

10

SYDNEY HEARD THE RAGGED panting of her attacker—Rabik, as she now knew—immediately behind her and felt his hot breath on her neck below the rim of her riding helmet. "Aargh!" she cried.

Little flashbulbs were going off somewhere behind her eyes, and she knew that it would only be a matter of moments before she lost consciousness. Gathering her strength, she rammed one elbow backward. She heard a pained *whoof* behind her as the blow connected, and the wire loosened slightly.

Using the momentary advantage, she reached up and yanked the wire loose. Rabik let out a furious curse and swung at her, but she knocked him aside with a well-placed kick and then jumped out of reach. Grabbing the handle of the riding crop that was tucked into her boot, she pulled it out and flicked the lever hidden at the end. The leather flew off, revealing the long, thin, very sharp blade hidden beneath.

Rabik's eyes widened in sudden fear as he saw the blade glint in the sunlight. But Sydney ignored him, stepping over to slash the trip wire with the blade.

When she turned around again to deal with the man, she gasped as she saw the muzzle of a gun pointed directly at her. "Hold it right there," Rabik croaked hoarsely. "Don't move."

Sydney froze. Dropping the blade, she slowly raised her hands, palms out.

Rabik smiled tightly. "That's better."

He stared at her for a second, keeping the gun trained on her. Then he glanced over toward Melanie, who was still lying motionless at the side of the course. Not hesitating, Sydney leaped into action, tumbling into the underbrush and behind a thick tree trunk.

A shot rang out, glancing off the bark just a few inches from her head. Chipper, who was now thrashing around in the underbrush nearby, let out another terrified scream and plunged straight toward where Sydney was hiding.

She gulped, realizing that the panicky horse's hooves could be just as deadly as the gun Rabik was holding.

Not giving herself a chance to think twice about the idea that had just popped into her head, she stood and grabbed at the gray's saddle as he bolted past. Calling upon every ounce of athleticism she possessed, she managed to grip the pommel of the saddle with one hand and the horse's mane with the other.

Her weight hanging off his right side seemed to add to Chipper's panic. He snorted and took off, leaping over the underbrush to land back on the course, just beyond the spot where Sydney had cut the wire.

"Hey!" Rabik's voice yelled out from somewhere nearby.

But Sydney didn't have any attention to spare for him. She was completely focused on hanging on as the horse skidded across the course and nearly went down. As he scrambled to regain his footing, Sydney managed to swing her left leg up and over the cantle of the saddle. She hooked her foot behind as the horse found his balance—and took off down the course at a dead gallop.

"Whoa!" Sydney gasped vainly as Chipper flattened out, gaining speed with every stride. She didn't dare look down at the ground flashing by beneath her—if she ended up there under his hooves, she was finished. In fact, she was already starting to think she might have had a better chance back with the gun.

Gritting her teeth, she focused on dragging herself farther into the saddle. She pulled herself up with the horse's mane, inch by inch, her muscles straining, until she was finally able to thrust her left leg over the horse. One last push and she found herself sitting upright in the saddle.

Almost immediately, the horse's wild gallop bounced her loose, nearly sending her flying off the saddle. Gasping for breath and blinking back the tears brought to her eyes by the air rushing past her, Sydney somehow managed to shove her feet into the stirrups. She then rose into a galloping position, resting her hands on the horse's withers and allowing her knees and ankles to absorb the shock of the rapid gait.

Only then did her mind start to work again. She glanced over her shoulder, but they had already left Rabik far behind.

Feeling the horse's weight shift, she turned to face front again, almost losing her balance as Chipper careened off the rope at the side of the course. He was still picking up speed as they neared a turn in the course, and Sydney almost shut her eyes in terror as she realized that if they didn't make the turn, they would end up tumbling down the steep ravine just ahead.

Instead, she grabbed the horse's right rein, yanking it out to the side. Chipper tossed his head in protest but slowed slightly, veering to the right and barely making the turn.

Before Sydney could exhale in relief, she saw the jump ahead of them. Less than twenty yards away, it was an enormous log that stretched across the course between two ancient trees. About a dozen onlookers were clustered on either side of the ropes watching their approach.

"Oh, no!" Sydney cried as the huge obstacle loomed closer with every stride. "Chipper, stop! *Stop!*"

She hauled back on the reins, but it was like trying to pull on a runaway freight train. The horse had the bit gripped in his teeth and his ears pricked forward as he spotted the jump. He lowered his head and charged on.

A few more strides, and they were almost on top of it. Several of the onlookers seemed to be shouting, but all Sydney could focus on was the feel of the horse's muscles gathering themselves as he threw himself onward and upward. She bent forward slightly to follow the motion, trying to recall her long-ago jump training.

"Aaaaaah!" she screamed as she was almost jarred loose on landing.

As Chipper raced on, Sydney was vaguely amazed that they had both made it over the jump in one piece, though she didn't have time to thank her lucky stars for that—she still had to deal with the runaway horse. Realizing that her riding helmet was still somehow, miraculously, on her head, Sydney took one hand off the reins and mane just long enough to snap the safety latch on the harness. Then she grabbed on again as her mount burst out of the woods, careening down a hill through a rolling meadow.

Spectators wandered here and there along the course. Sydney wondered if anyone realized yet that something was wrong—Melanie's accident and her own struggle with Rabik had only taken a few moments, and she supposed that anyone who wasn't watching carefully might not even notice that Chipper had the wrong rider.

Then again, maybe they would, Sydney thought grimly as Chipper drifted to the left, almost grazing the rope boundary again before straightening himself out. *I'm not exactly riding like I'm ready for the next Olympics here. . . .*

Glancing ahead, she saw that they were approaching another jump. This one was a gigantic table jump, as wide as it was high, set in a slight dip in the ground. If Sydney had thought the log jump was big, this one seemed at least twice as huge. Fear stabbed her heart as she imagined trying to stay on over something like.

"Oh, no," she muttered fiercely, gathering up the reins. "We're definitely not doing that again."

Chipper had spotted the jump, too. Once again, his ears pricked as he locked onto it. He galloped on, barely seeming to notice as Sydney pulled back on the reins for all she was worth.

"Chipper!" she yelled. "Come on, stop! Whoa!"

Still the horse kept going. Changing her tactics, Sydney pulled on the left rein only, hoping at least to turn the horse around the jump.

But Chipper had other ideas. Charging forward, he headed straight for the jump. They were only four strides away, then three, then two...

As she felt Chipper's haunches gather for take-off, Sydney gave one last, desperate yank on the reins. But all she managed to do was throw Chipper off balance—as he left the ground, she felt him wobble and lurch to the left.

"Urgh!" she grunted as the horse's front hooves landed on the flat, solid top of the jump, the impact jerking her forward onto his neck.

Before she could regain her seat he flung himself forward, scrabbling for a hold with his hind legs. He finally managed to find a foothold on the tabletop and launched himself forward off the other side.

Time seemed to shift into slow motion. Sydney was flung backward and to the side as the horse flew through the air. Both of her feet flew out of the stirrups, so the only things holding her on were her right leg, which was hooked over the saddle, and her right hand, buried in Chipper's mane. She heard the spectators gasp loudly. Realizing she was about to come off, she glanced down, hoping to gauge her landing spot.

Drop, tuck, and roll, she thought as Chipper's forelegs hit the ground, almost jarring her loose. Her glance showed her not only a dizzying glimpse of the hard ground, but also a split-second view of the faces of the few closest spectators. One all-too-familiar face leaped out at her—it was the vet she'd seen with Lawton and Rabik! He was staring at her, holding what appeared to be a walkie-talkie to his mouth.

Sydney gulped, not daring to imagine what

would happen if she hit the ground at his feet. Clinging on to the mane, she hauled herself forward as Chipper galloped off again.

". . . and there seems to be some kind of problem at the tabletop." The announcer's voice floated over the scene as Sydney clenched her teeth, her muscles burning as she once again pulled herself into the saddle. *"Melanie Lawton was nearly unseated when her horse banked the jump, and appears now to be struggling hard to stay on board. . . ."*

This time when she fished for her stirrups she could only find one. The other seemed to have flown off somewhere over the table jump. The first was flapping against Chipper's side, which seemed to be getting him even more excited. He threw in a little buck as he ran, almost unseating Sydney yet again.

"Don't you dare!" she shouted at the horse, scrabbling for the reins and catching them just before they flew forward out of reach. She gathered them up as the horse reached the edge of the meadow and galloped through a break in the line of trees. Before them lay the main part of the course, which was dotted with jumps. Less than two hundred yards away Sydney could see the bustling vendor area near the entrance and dressage rings.

Meanwhile, another obstacle was already in

view on the course just ahead, this one a sturdy post and rail jump on a slight incline. Narrowing her eyes with determination, Sydney clung to the horse's sides with her legs and leaned to the left, at the same time dragging the left rein back to her hip.

"If you won't stop, at least you can go where I tell you," Sydney muttered grimly under her breath.

This time the horse couldn't ignore her cues. Though he shook his head in irritation, he allowed her to steer him off to the left. He hit the rope at the edge of the course and broke through it, sending the people on the other side scattering with screams of terror. Sydney's eyes widened as she saw a stout, gray-haired woman sitting on a folding chair at the end of the jump, holding a clipboard.

Fortunately Chipper saw her, too. He veered sharply, managing to barely miss running over the woman.

Wanting to minimize the potential mayhem, Sydney yanked on the right rein to steer Chipper back on course. As he broke through the rope barrier again, he almost tripped on the ends flapping around beneath his legs. His pace slowed slightly as he fought for his balance, and Sydney took advantage, pulling back on the reins.

Now that she was back in the populated area of the grounds, all she could think about was getting the horse stopped so she could jump off and disappear into the crowd. Her mind racing ahead even as she seesawed the reins to slow the horse, she quickly formulated a plan. As soon as she hit the ground, she would activate the search signal set into her fingernail. If the wild ride hadn't broken it, it would let Noah know that there was a problem. Once the two of them found each other, they could take off for the airport immediately. There was no question in her mind that it was time to pull out— even if Lawton hadn't been on to her before, he definitely would be now.

"Okay, Chipper, take it easy," she murmured as the horse's gallop slowed to a brisk canter. "That's right, all done."

She tugged on the reins again, hoping to bring the horse down to a trot. Instead, Chipper's ears flattened back against his head. Before Sydney could react, he let out several quick, hard bucks.

The reins flew out of Sydney's hands again as she desperately clung on with her legs, trying to keep her seat. She grabbed his mane with one hand and one of the flopping reins with the other. Giving the rein a yank, she almost unbalanced herself, and wound up accidentally kicking Chipper in the flank with her left leg.

The horse's head shot straight up in alarm, and

he leaped forward. Sydney pulled again on the rein, sending the horse screeching to the left. He burst through the course rope and onto the grass, once again sending the crowd scattering. This time Sydney squeezed her eyes shut, not daring to look as the horse plunged across the crowded grounds, bucking and squealing.

There were screams and shouts from every side, but the sickening thud or crunch or splat she was waiting for didn't come. Opening her eyes, she screamed as she saw a hot dog cart directly in front of them.

The hot dog seller dove for the ground as Chipper launched himself, leaping straight over the metal cart. He landed hard on the other side, and Sydney hit the front of the saddle even harder, the air whooshing out of her body on impact.

When she looked up again a second later, she saw with relief that the ground just ahead of them was clear of people. Chipper was galloping down a broad dirt lane between two rows of food vendors.

Then her eyes widened as she realized that they were now heading straight for a long, rickety-looking wooden dock at the edge of a marshy pond. She had noted the area during her explorations the day before—the pond was lined with picnic tables and was home to several placid ducks.

"Chipper, no!" she cried, lunging for the reins.

But this time it was too late. The horse hit the end of the dock and threw up his head as his hooves hit the strange surface. He tried to stop, but momentum sent him skittering forward over the rough boards. As he twisted, trying desperately to remain upright, Sydney felt herself part ways with the saddle once and for all. She flew off to the left side, tumbling head over heels through the air.

A moment later she splashed into the pond. Ducks scattered before her, a blur of feathers in her eyes as her head fell back and soundly smacked one of the dock's wooden pilings.

Then everything went dark.

11

SYDNEY CHOKED AND GASPED for breath, realizing that her mouth was filled with sour-tasting water. She sat up woozily, spitting out the water and shaking her head to try to clear it of the cobwebs that seemed to have filled it.

For a few seconds she couldn't remember who she was, or where. All she could focus on was the raw, throbbing pain at the back of her skull.

She gradually became aware of the cold water seeping into every pore of her body, and of anxious shouting from somewhere nearby. She blinked, wondering why she couldn't seem to see anything.

When she reached for her face, her fingers touched sopping wet velvet.

She pushed back the brim of her riding helmet, which had fallen forward over her eyes, and suddenly everything came back at once. Sitting abruptly upright, she ignored the dizziness and the flash of nausea that hit her as she glanced around.

Her helmet immediately slipped down again, blocking much of her view, but she could see that she was sitting in about two feet of swampy water at the base of the dock. Nearby, she caught a glimpse of Chipper's muddy gray legs as he jumped out of the little pond and trotted away. A buzz of murmurs and shouts rose all around her, and closer than any of it she heard hurried footsteps on the dock just overhead.

"Never mind," an authoritative male voice rang out suddenly from somewhere close by. "Stand back, give her air. Everything's under control. Please stand back—I'm going to take her to the medic's tent. She'll be okay. Please let us through."

A moment later Sydney saw two sets of legs clad in dark trousers splashing through the water toward her. She squinted, fuzzily trying to figure out why the legs looked so familiar.

Of course, she realized a second later, smiling

happily to have remembered. *Noah was wearing those tan pants today. It must be Noah coming to rescue me.* She blinked, looking again at the approaching legs. One, two, three, four legs . . . *I guess I must've hit my head pretty hard—I'm seeing double.*

The legs reached her, and she felt strong arms grasp her under her armpits and haul her up. A second set of hands grabbed her ankles, and Sydney allowed her body to go limp as her unseen rescuers carried her out of the pond. Her head throbbed with the motion, but she did her best to ignore it.

Maybe next Noah will help me take off this darn helmet so I can see again, Sydney thought, her mind still hazy. *I guess he's probably waiting to do that until we're safely in the car on our way back to the hotel.*

Even through a sudden, almost paralyzing sense of weariness, she felt a rush of gratitude for her partner. Noah might be overbearing at times, he might be a bit arrogant and touchy, he might drive her crazy. But he always came through for her in the end. How many times had he rescued her or otherwise saved the day on their missions together? She couldn't remember, but she suspected it was a lot.

I guess maybe I shouldn't have teased him about

me saving him in France, Sydney thought, letting her eyes drift closed as she was carried through the crowd. *Maybe I should apologize for that. . . .*

She opened her mouth to speak. Before she could, she felt herself being flung through the air. A second later her body thudded painfully against a hard, unyielding surface.

"Hey!" she blurted out hoarsely, her eyes flying open just in time to see a large metal door swing shut in front of her with a loud clang. She pushed herself up on her elbows, prickly bits of straw grinding into her skin.

Adrenaline and fear shooed the last few fuzzy wisps from her mind. Yanking off her helmet so she could see clearly, she glanced around. Dim light coming through windows crusted over with dirt showed her that she was in the back of a large horse trailer. There were three narrow stalls across the front of the truck, two of which were occupied by horses. Sydney was in the back section of the truck. The stall dividers there had been folded back against the side, leaving a large open area.

She scrambled to her feet and leaped toward the door. But just as she reached it, she heard a clang as it was bolted from the outside. She flung herself against it, but the door didn't budge.

She stared around wildly, almost losing her balance as the trailer jerked into motion. She heard a horse scrambling for balance in the stall behind her.

Grabbing the wall for support, Sydney glanced back at the horses. The one on the far right had been backed into the stall and was facing her, its head weaving from side to side and its eyes rolling nervously. It let out an earsplitting scream of protest, and a second later there was a loud clang as it kicked out at the stall wall. Sydney's eyes widened as she recognized the horse's distinctive crooked white blaze.

"Rocket!" she breathed in surprise, her mind spinning. What did this mean? Why was she suddenly trapped in a horse trailer with Melanie's mare?

She glanced at the other horse, which was standing quietly in the left-hand stall. It was facing away from her, but when she took a step closer she quickly recognized the heaving, sweating, mud-flecked gray flanks—not to mention the saddle that was still strapped to the horse's back. It was Chipper!

As she turned in confusion to glance at Rocket once more, she saw that the mare wasn't alone in her stall. A man was at her side, his left hand resting on her shoulder as he moved forward and back with the restless mare. Even in the dim light from the windows, Sydney instantly recognized the vet she'd seen with Lawton and Rabik the day before. He didn't even seem to notice her presence as he raised his right hand to the light, revealing that it was holding a syringe.

"Hey!" Sydney shouted, leaping toward the man. "What are you doing here? Where am I? Where are we going?"

The man spun to face her. "Who are you?" he blurted out, clearly startled. "What are you doing in here?"

"That's what I want to know!" Sydney growled, grabbing him and yanking him out of the stall by his shirt collar. "Now start talking!"

As the man's shoulder hit her, Rocket's eyes rolled back in her head, and she half-reared in her stall. When she landed on all fours again, she kicked out three or four times, the echoing blows drowning out the vet's response. But the fury in his eyes was clear enough.

He twisted his left elbow around, knocking Sydney's grip loose. Then he spun and swung at her.

She blocked the blow and kicked out at him. He dodged the blow with his free hand but fell backward, collapsing against the metal guard that was keeping Rocket in her stall. His weight was too much for the flimsy chain and it broke, sending him falling with a grunt onto the hard metal floor at the mare's feet.

Rocket let out another scream and reared again, higher this time, her hooves waving above the fallen man. The vet's eyes widened in terror, and he shoved himself aside just in time as the mare's feet crashed down where he had been lying. In the other stall, Chipper shifted his weight and snorted, his hooves thumping against the floor.

Sydney jumped forward, striking the man hard in the face as he leaped to his feet. He staggered and almost fell again, grabbing the edge of the stall divider with both hands to catch himself. The syringe he'd been holding went flying, bounced on the floor, and lodged against a dried clump of manure. The vet jumped toward it, but Sydney blocked him, shoving him back against the metal wall. As he slid partway to the floor, his right leg shot out, catching Sydney by surprise and bringing her down.

"Oof!" she grunted as she fell heavily into the opposite wall.

Meanwhile, Rocket had just figured out that there was nothing holding her in her stall anymore. Tossing her head, she plunged past the broken stall guard and skidded across the unbedded metal floor of the open area.

"Aaah!" the vet cried, throwing himself to the side just in time as the mare lost her balance, crashed into the wall, and almost went down.

Sydney ducked beneath the stall guard blocking the empty center stall, her heart pounding as Rocket crashed around the claustrophobic space in the back of the trailer. The mare's sleek body was lathered with sweat, and the dank scent filled the trailer, the raw smell of fear. Chipper had spun around in his stall and was stretching his head out over the chain, calling to the mare uncertainly, though she ignored him.

This is not good, Sydney thought grimly as Rocket let out another loud scream and kicked out at the wall. *Not good at all.*

Just then the trailer made a sharp turn, throwing them all off balance. As Sydney grabbed the divider for support, the mare flung out her legs, trying to stay upright. The vet took advantage of the horse's momentary pause to dart forward and grab her halter.

"Get up!" he shouted at her. "Come on, you worthless brumby!"

The mare threw her head up but allowed the man to turn her. A moment later Sydney's eyes widened as she saw the horse barreling straight toward her. Moving fast, the vet used his free hand to yank open one end of the stall guard, his eyes gleaming with malice as he stared at Sydney.

Sydney leaped forward just in time, pushing past the horse as Rocket leaped into the stall. Momentum sent Sydney crashing against the rear doors of the trailer; then she turned her head and saw the vet hooking the stall chain to contain the nervous mare.

As she stepped toward him, her foot hit something small and light, sending it skittering across the floor. Glancing down, she saw that it was the syringe.

The vet saw it too, and dove for it, rolling under the stall guard and grabbing it just before one of Rocket's forefeet landed on it. Then he rolled quickly to the side to avoid the horse's deadly, dancing hooves.

This time Sydney leaped at him as soon as he was out of the stall, pinning him to the floor with her weight before he could get up again. She kneeled on his upper arms, her hands on his throat.

"Start talking," she hissed. "Tell me where this trailer is going."

The vet smiled. "I have . . . a better . . . idea," he said, his words choked by the pressure of her hands.

Sydney blinked, confused. A second later she

gasped as she felt a sharp jab in her left thigh. Glancing down, she saw the man's thumb pressing down the plunger of the syringe.

Sedative, Sydney realized as a heavy feeling flooded through her body. *That's what he was doing—he was tranquilizing the horses for the trip. . . .*

She didn't have time to take the thought any further. A fog of darkness worked its way through her mind, and her muscles all seemed to detach from one another. A moment later she slumped to the floor, unconscious.

12

"UGH," SYDNEY MOANED UNDER her breath as she swam toward consciousness. She couldn't believe those frat-boy jerks who lived downstairs—why did they have to crank up the bass on their stereo so loud whenever they had a party? She was going to have to sic Francie on them again. . . .

The steady throbbing rhythm filled her head and her entire body until it seemed that even her heart was beating in time. As Sydney's senses slowly returned, she realized something strange: there was no music, just the beat.

With some effort, she opened her eyes, which

felt as if they'd been sealed shut with sticky molasses. At first what she saw made no sense at all to her muddled mind—gray walls, gray ceiling, gray light . . . Where were their cheerful striped curtains, Francie's movie-star posters and her clothes and makeup strewn all over the place?

Sydney's muscles tensed, causing her left thigh to spasm painfully. With that, it all came flooding back—Australia, the mission, the battle in the horse trailer. Her heart skipped a beat as she realized she had no idea how much time had passed since the horse tranquilizer had knocked her out.

Keeping her eyes half closed in case anyone was watching her, she did her best to scan the area without moving. She definitely wasn't on that trailer anymore. But where was she? Spotting a cabinet door labeled PARACHUTES, she realized that she had to be aboard a plane. The throbbing rhythm was the powerful engine.

She moved her head slightly to one side to get a better view. Behind her, she saw a cargo hold lined with stalls. Rocket's familiar head was hanging out over one of the doors, her eyes dull and sleepy. Chipper and two other horses were looking out of their stalls as well. The sounds of shifting hooves blended with the dull roar of the plane.

Then Sydney heard another sound: human voices.

She strained her ears, trying to sift the murmur of the voices from the other noises. The speakers were nearby, though she couldn't see them. She closed her eyes to help herself hear better.

". . . and I thought that idiot mare was going to kill herself and me too," one voice grumbled. "They might have warned me they were throwing that Seppo in with me—bloody sheila knocked the needle right out of my hand before I knew she was there, and I had to knock her out and then go fossicking around the horse box to find it again."

Sydney grimaced as she recognized the voice of the vet. His version of events didn't quite match what she remembered, but she figured that was the least of her problems at the moment.

"Never mind, mate." The second voice was deeper and gruffer. "The mare is here now, and that's what matters."

"Right. And we've got the bloody gray as well—we'll just see what Lawton has to say about that when he finds out."

"Don't worry about Lawton." The second voice was cold and hard. "Now if you quit yabbering and get to work, you can get the chips implanted before we're halfway to the coast, and then the pair of them will be ready to go on with the others."

"Reckon." The vet sounded slightly annoyed. "I'll just get to it, then."

Sydney kept her eyes closed, trying to figure out what she was hearing. Her mind was still slightly groggy from the sedative, but she forced herself to focus. Implanting a chip? What was that all about?

Suddenly an image of the computer lab in Lawton's house flashed into her mind's eye. Of course! The men had to be talking about a computer chip. Maybe they were implanting microchips in Rocket and the other horses for identification purposes. But if that was all they were doing, why all the skulking around? It just didn't make sense.

She could hear the men moving around somewhere very close by. Cracking one eye open slightly, she almost gasped aloud as a familiar form loomed over her. It was Rabik!

He stepped over her without a downward glance and hurried into the stall area, where he paused in front of Rocket. Then he looked back toward his companion.

"She's ready for you, mate," he called. "Don't worry, she's not in any state to put up much of a fight anymore." Through her slitted eye, Sydney saw him glance in her direction. "Kind of like that one, eh?"

She heard the vet laugh. "I hope I didn't overdo it," he said. Not wanting the men to know that she was awake, Sydney closed her eye as he walked toward her and looked down. She felt his toe nudge her in the side. "Figured she might just be of some use to us alive."

"Maybe." Rabik sounded dubious. "Long as we don't wind up dragging her all the way to Europe with us. Too risky."

At that moment the sound of a hoof striking solid wood rang through the hold. With a low oath, Rabik turned toward Rocket, who was looking slightly more alert. Sydney felt a slight whoosh of air as the vet stepped over her.

"Let's get this done," the vet said. "Don't know why the boss was so determined for us to take this one, anyhow. She's been more trouble than she's worth—there are plenty of other horses around that would've done in her place."

Cracking her eye open again, Sydney saw Rabik shrug. "Don't ask me," he said to his companion, who was fiddling with a small canvas bag that appeared to hold medical equipment. "Think Lawton just wanted to make sure his girl didn't go back to riding her—he never did trust this mare, not since she dumped Melanie that time and broke her ribs."

"Well, I just hope the bloody brumby doesn't end up blowing the whole lurk," the vet grumbled. "If this mare kicks up a fuss at customs, people are more likely to look closer at her—and the rest of them. More likely to notice something's amiss."

"Not if you do your job right," Rabik responded sharply. "No matter how closely they look, they won't know what's really going on—not unless they X-ray her entire body and spot that chip. And they're not going to do that. This batch will go through, just like the last batch and the one before that. And no one will be the wiser, especially once the horses are scattered across the continent in their new homes."

"Yeah," the vet said. "Unless someone notices that almost all the horses you and Lawton ship overseas have an unexplained scar somewhere on them. Small or no, there's no way to hide it completely. I keep telling the boss, we have to be careful not to overdo this or someone's bound to notice."

Rabik glared at him. "There are people wanting the information on these chips," he growled. "People who aren't willing to wait, and who are willing to pay plenty for what we're sending them. That's worth a little risk, I'd say." He shrugged. "Besides, what horse that's knocked around a cross-country course a time or two doesn't have some kind of scar somewhere? As long as you vary the location, it's no drama."

Sydney's mind was getting clearer all the time, and what she was hearing was starting to make sense. *Lawton and his pals must implant computer chips beneath the skin of all these horses they're shipping to Europe and Malaysia,* she thought, re-calling the shipping addresses she'd seen in Law-ton's office. *Then once they arrive—maybe even while they're still in quarantine—someone on that end removes the chips and gets them into the hands of whatever terrorists or other criminals have paid for the information on them. No one would suspect that anyone would use expensive performance horses for smuggling, so no one is ever the wiser. Especially since Lawton has the perfect excuse for all this horse trading—his daughter.*

She couldn't help feeling a flash of admiration for Lawton's ingenuity. The plan was a complicated and time-consuming way of smuggling dangerous black-market information, but it was also safe and close to foolproof. This was exactly what she and Noah had come to Australia to learn.

She peeked at the men again. The vet was step-ping into Rocket's stall as Rabik watched.

"Wonder what Melanie will do when she realizes dear Daddy sold this mare out from under her?" the vet called from inside the stall. "Not to mention the gray . . ."

Rabik shrugged. "What can she do?" he said. "She'll be in hospital for a week or two at minimum. By the time she gets out, the pair of them will be long gone. I'm sure Lawton will use the accident as an excuse—what can she say against a worried father? Besides, she's got plenty of others to bring along. She'll never be the wiser, and life will go on as usual."

Sydney winced with sympathy for Melanie. The man's words confirmed that Lawton's daughter had no idea about the racket her father was running. *So much for that close father-daughter bond,* she thought grimly.

"Yeah, s'pose you're right, mate," the vet responded. "The only thing that could muck us up this time is that nosy sheila out there. What're we going to do about her, anyway?"

Sydney's body tensed as she realized he was referring to her. She listened carefully.

"Good question." Rabik's voice hardened. "From what I hear, the folks over at K-D would pay big money to get their hands on this one."

K-D? Sydney guessed that could only mean K-

Directorate. Sydney's heart sank as she realized what that meant—her captors had figured out her true identity. That meant she was in even more trouble than she'd thought.

Her blood ran cold as she heard Rabik's next words: "Then again, that sort of bizzo might just be more trouble than it's worth. Might be better off to kill her right now."

13

SYONEY'S HEART THUODEO IN her chest as Rabik's words echoed in her ears. She had to escape. But how?

Trying not to move enough to attract the men's attention, she cautiously felt around herself. Her pockets had been emptied; her riding helmet was long gone, along with her blond Tammy Rae wig; and the only piece of spy equipment she had left was her camera belt. Well, that and the rhinestone signaling device embedded in her fingernail. She squinted at it, wondering if it still worked after her wild ride and subsequent dunking. Even if it did, she remembered Graham's warning that it had only been tested up to a range of about fifty miles.

"Want to give me a hand in here, mate?" the vet grunted from inside Rocket's stall. "Doped up or not, this one's still not going to make things easy on me."

Rabik sighed. "All right," he said, opening the stall door and stepping inside.

Sydney took advantage of their distraction to quietly roll toward the nearest plane window. Pushing herself to her knees and doing her best to ignore the rubbery feeling in her limbs, she peered outside and down.

All she could see was red. Sun-baked red sand stretched from horizon to horizon, only an occasional hill or scrub tree breaking its monotonous expanse. Sydney immediately knew that they had to be flying over the Australian outback, specifically the immense inland desert known as the Red Center, which covered nearly two hundred thousand square miles in the middle of the continent, with only a few dusty roads connecting the widely spread homesteads and cattle stations.

She glanced toward the front of the plane and its unseen pilot, wondering if she could somehow force him or her to land the plane down there on the sand. *At least on the ground I might have a fighting chance,* Sydney thought grimly.

She heard the sudden blow of hoof against wood, and a muffled curse. Glancing toward Rocket's stall, she saw the mare tossing her head wildly and guessed that the men would have their hands full for at least a few more minutes.

It's now or never, she told herself.

The mare kicked again and whinnied frantically, and the men shouted instructions at each other. Sydney crawled quickly back toward the narrow aisle that ran the length of one side of the plane, the sound of her movements lost in the commotion. First she needed to find herself something—anything—to use as a weapon. She tried to rip loose a metal railing along the aisle leading toward the cockpit, but it was attached too tightly. As she crawled past the parachute cabinet she'd noticed earlier, she clicked open the door and scanned the interior, but all that was inside was the soft cloth and lines of the parachutes.

As she turned to check that her captors were still busy with the horse, her gaze fell on the vet's bag, which he'd left open in the middle of the stall aisle with its contents spilling out. In addition to a stethoscope, various bandages, and other veterinary equipment, she spotted a plastic Baggie holding several computer chips.

With a quick glance toward Rocket's stall, Sydney stood and darted toward the bag. Stuffing the Baggie into her pocket, she scrabbled through the rest of the medical bag's contents, hoping to find a scalpel or anything else she could use as a weapon.

Suddenly there was another shouted curse from the vet. "This is ridiculous!" he cried. "Rabik, go out and grab the big needle from my bag. We'll have to give her another hit, or she'll kill us both."

Sydney dashed around the corner and stood with her back pressed against the wall, hoping against hope that Rabik wouldn't think to glance toward the spot where she had been lying. As she held her breath and listened, her eyes wandered toward the small alcove across the aisle, which held a refrigerator and a tiny table bolted to the floor.

Her heart jumped. The galley!

There was another crash and curse from the hold, and the sound of running footsteps assured her that she was the last thing on the men's minds at the moment. Dashing across to the little galley, she pulled open the first drawer she came to.

"Bingo," she whispered under her breath, staring down at the assortment of kitchen utensils inside.

Selecting the largest, sharpest-looking knife in the drawer, she turned and peered back out into the aisle. The only sounds were still coming from the stall area.

Sydney crept out into the aisle and turned toward the front of the plane. The cockpit door was closed but not latched. She paused at it, pressing her ear to the metal and listening. There was no sound from within, and thus no way of telling how many people might be inside. She was just going to have to wing it.

Gripping the knife tightly in one hand, she silently twisted the door handle and pulled it open. Then she leaped into the cockpit and, in one smooth move practiced a hundred times in her training, grabbed the back of the pilot's chair with her left arm and with the other hand pressed the blade of her knife against his throat.

"Hey!" The pilot, a swarthy man in his fifties, tried to leap up but stopped short when he felt the cold steel bite into his skin.

"Not so fast," Sydney hissed into his ear. "One shout to your friends, and it's slice and dice time."

"Fine, okay," the pilot said in a New Zealand accent. "Don't do anything crazy, Ms. Bristow."

Sydney was momentarily startled that the pilot knew her real name, but she didn't let it throw off her focus. "I want you to land this plane right now, as fast as you can."

The pilot rolled his eyes back, trying to give her an incredulous look. "Right here in the middle of the Never Never?" he said. "I'm afraid that's not a very good idea."

"I don't care what you think!" Sydney snapped, all too aware that the men in the back could notice her disappearance at any moment. "Just do it. Or I'll just have to put you out of your misery and land this thing myself."

She shot a worried glance at the control panel, wondering if she could follow through if the pilot called her bluff. Part of her training had involved learning to operate all sorts of transportation, but she hadn't had much real-world experience at flying beyond a few quick spins around the local airstrip in a one-engine plane.

How hard could it be? she reassured herself, gripping the knife tightly. *Considering the alternatives . . .*

"Aha!"

Before Sydney could react, she felt a rough blow to her right shoulder. Her entire arm went numb for a moment, and the knife clattered out of her grip and onto the control panel before bouncing to the floor and out of sight.

Sydney gasped in astonishment and spun around just in time to duck Rabik's swinging fist. The momentum of his blow sent him staggering off-balance with a curse, and Sydney leaped past him and through the cockpit doorway before he could recover.

Five strides brought her down the length of the aisle and back into the cargo hold, where she almost ran into an astonished-looking vet. "Hey!" he yelled. "She's back here!"

Sydney saw him reach down just long enough to grab a syringe out of the bag on the floor. She took a step toward him and kicked out fiercely, sending the vet spinning around and the syringe flying off into one of the stalls.

Wheeling around, she was just in time to see Rabik flying toward her down the aisle with a twisted grimace on his face and the kitchen knife clenched in his fist.

Sydney jumped toward him and blocked his blow as he tried to plunge the knife into her chest. Using his own weight and momentum against him, she grabbed his arm and sent him flying face-first into the plane's metal escape hatch door with a grunt of pain, his shoulder just missing the lever that opened the hatch.

Meanwhile, the effort of the move almost sent Sydney crumpling to her knees. She gasped for breath and bent over, realizing that the sedative was still affecting her. With its lingering effects in her system, there was no way she would be able to fight off all three men for long.

Looking up, she saw that the cockpit door was slightly ajar. One against one seemed like much better odds than one against three—maybe she could lock herself in there. Then all she would have to do was take out the pilot and figure out how to land the plane herself. She wasn't sure what would happen after that, but she decided to take things one step at a time.

Gathering her strength, she darted down the aisle just as she heard Rabik climb to his feet. She jumped into the cockpit and turned to yank the door shut, but her hand slid off the handle as the pilot grabbed her from behind, wrapping his arms around her torso and pinning her arms at her sides.

Sydney struggled against him and finally managed to snap his hold on her arms. But by then it was too late—both Rabik and the vet were pushing through the cockpit doorway with expressions of rage on their faces. Rabik's nose was bleeding profusely, and the vet had retrieved his syringe and was holding it at the ready.

"Get her," Rabik snarled at the pilot. "Hold her down. And this time let's make sure she's going to sleep forever."

Sydney spun around to protect herself, but the pilot landed a blow on her chest, and she felt herself fly backward until her spine met painfully with the plane's control panel.

For a second she thought she must have hit her head, too, because the entire cockpit seemed to tilt woozily to one side. Then she heard the men shouting fearfully, along with a sickening screech of air outside and muffled cries from the horses in the back of the plane. She realized that she must have bumped the steering column on the panel, sending the plane into a sharp nosedive!

She felt herself shoved roughly aside as the men leaped toward the panel to regain control. Hitting the floor hard, Sydney felt her head snap back and hit the side of the control panel. But she fought off the momentary pain and nausea resulting from the blow and skittered toward the doorway.

"Hey! Stop her!"

She ignored the shout from behind her and sprinted down the short aisle. She had no idea where she was heading—but it wasn't in her nature to give up. There had to be a way out of this. All she had to do was find it.

She skidded to a stop beside the galley, wondering if she could dash in and grab another knife before the men caught up to her. As she spun around to see how close they were, the bright lettering of the parachute cabinet caught her eye.

Her breath caught in her throat as a crazy idea popped into her mind. She couldn't . . .

"Grab her!" Rabik's furious voice echoed down the aisle. "Out of my way!"

She sensed rather than saw his bulk flinging itself toward her. Moving fast, she snapped open the cabinet and grabbed a parachute from inside. Then she spun around just in time to dodge Rabik as he swung at her with both fists.

The vet was right behind Rabik. "Check it out, mate," he said with a laugh. "The sheila is going to fight us off with a chute."

Rabik grinned horribly in response. "Nice choice," he said, grabbing at the parachute Sydney was holding in front of her like a shield. "Now the only decision is should we use it to strangle her or to smother her?"

"How about neither?" Sydney snarled at him.

In one swift motion she turned and kicked at

the lever on the escape hatch. The door flew open, and instantly the air outside howled into the plane, causing the men to stagger back and the horses to scream again. Sydney was vaguely aware of the two men scrabbling for a hold to avoid being swept out of the plane.

Meanwhile, she clutched the parachute to her chest and, without allowing herself even a split second of hesitation, leaped out through the hatch into the open air.

14

SYDNEY'S SHOULDER MUSCLES SCREAMED in protest as she twisted them into impossible positions, trying desperately to yank the parachute harness over her arms. The air whistled in her ears and brought tears to her eyes as she tumbled head over heels through the thin air, making it difficult to hear or see or even think.

She glanced down and saw the dull red expanse of the outback far below. How far had she already fallen—a hundred yards, two hundred, three? Tearing her gaze away, she gave another tug on the parachute. If she could just get it in place, she might be able to pull the ripcord in time. . . .

Just as one of the straps finally slid over her left elbow, a shadow suddenly fell over her from somewhere immediately overhead. For a moment she thought it was the plane returning. But a split second later she felt a violent yank on the other parachute strap. She gasped, wanting to shout in protest, but the wind grabbed her words and ripped them away before her ears could register them.

A quick glance upward confirmed her worst fear . . . she wasn't the only one plummeting toward the ground. She was staring straight into the snarling face of one of the men from the plane—Rabik! Sydney gasped as his elbow connected solidly with her left cheekbone. She felt the parachute slip down her arm as he grabbed for it again. He must have lost his balance during their struggle and fallen out after her.

And now he wanted her parachute.

Sydney snatched the parachute strap just before it slipped off over her fingers. Holding on tightly with one hand, she reached up and grabbed at Rabik's hand, which was gripping one of the other straps. Glancing up, she saw that he was shouting something at her, his face twisted with rage, but she couldn't hear it. The wind in her ears was almost deafening now.

She raked her long fake fingernails across his skin as hard as she could. She felt one or two of the nails break off, but she didn't stop scratching until she felt Rabik's grip loosen. But another quick glance up showed that he held on to the top of the parachute case with his other hand.

Gritting her teeth, Sydney clenched the strap with both hands. Every muscle in her body strained as she pulled herself up until she could get her right elbow through it. Then she held on tightly and swung her legs up, trying to kick Rabik away. But gravity was working against her, and her left foot barely grazed his side.

A split second later she gasped as she felt him latch onto her ankle. "Let go of me!" she yelled, even though she knew he probably couldn't hear her. She tried to yank her foot away, but he clung to it firmly, and her tight riding boots didn't slip even an inch. Sydney gasped with pain as she felt him bite down on her knee just above the top of the boot. Her grip on the strap slipped as she struggled to get her leg away from him, but luckily her elbow remained threaded through the strap.

Finally Sydney managed to kick her free leg up

far enough to connect with some part of her attacker. She wasn't sure where she'd hit him, but she felt his grip loosen immediately. Peering upward, she noted with satisfaction that blood was flying out of his mouth and at least one of his front teeth seemed to have disappeared.

One last yank pulled her foot free, and Sydney felt her body spin out to the side, almost causing her to lose the parachute again. Then she felt a yank, and a look up at Rabik showed that he was pulling himself down over the parachute with his arms wrapped around the case. As she watched, he inched himself further, clutching on tightly to his quarry.

Sydney's heart froze with terror. If he managed to pull himself just a little farther, he would have enough leverage to yank the straps out of her grip, and it would all be over.

She tried to kick out at him again, but the paralyzing air pressure stymied her efforts—she couldn't quite get enough momentum to swing herself straight up at him. Meanwhile Rabik was inching closer and closer over the top of the parachute, his eyes glittering with malice and triumph.

Sydney scowled at him. They were almost face to face now, so close that she could see the loose skin of Rabik's jowls fluttering in the pressure of the air rushing upward past him.

She had to do something. Though she didn't dare glance down, she knew that if one of them didn't deploy the parachute soon, it would be too late for both of them. Doing the only thing she could think of, she pursed her lips—and spit straight into Rabik's face.

Rabik was caught off guard as the gob of saliva smacked him square in the left eye. His head jerked back, and suddenly he was flying off to one side, somersaulting wildly in midair, until Sydney lost sight of him in the white-hot glare of the sun. This time Sydney could hear him howling in terror as she and the parachute skittered away, the force of her efforts to hold on to it sending her tumbling head over heels until she wasn't sure which way was up.

As she flipped around again and again, she felt the parachute strap start to slip down her right arm toward her hand. The forces of the air pressure and of gravity were so strong that she couldn't swing her other arm around in time, so all she could do was grapple desperately with her right hand. . . . But a second later she felt it slip off and away.

Sydney looked up and saw the parachute start

to drift away from her. Instantly summoning all the strength she had left, she flung her body into a flip. Her long legs flew up above her head—and she hooked one of the parachute's flying straps with one foot.

There was no time for so much as a sigh of relief. Sydney grabbed the parachute, and still not daring to look down, she managed to yank it on over her shoulders. Not wasting the extra seconds to buckle it across her chest, she quickly located the pull string and yanked it.

A second later she felt a sudden pull on her entire body as the parachute deployed and filled with air. She nearly went limp with relief but clung tightly to the shoulder straps with both hands as she fell through the air beneath the billowing cloud of red and white fabric.

Finally she looked down—and almost wished she hadn't. The solid red expanse of the ground was terrifyingly close, and she was still falling way too fast. It was going to be a rough landing. . . .

She took a few deep breaths as the ground rushed closer and closer. Focusing on her legs, she willed them to become limp and flexible.

When she hit, she let her knees and ankles crumple beneath her to absorb some of the impact. Still, the massive force of the landing spun her forward onto the ground. She felt her right cheekbone being scraped raw and her torso bumping off of sharp rocks as the parachute dragged her over the sand.

When she finally skidded to a stop and heard the parachute come down somewhere in front of her, she almost hugged the ground with relief. She pushed herself slowly into a sitting position, testing each limb before she moved it. She had scrapes and cuts all over her face and body, her clothes were cut to ribbons, and she was sure her entire body would be one giant bruise once the shock wore off. But she still seemed to be in one piece.

She climbed to her feet with a groan. After a moment of fumbling, she managed to pull the parachute harness off her chest. A glance upward showed no sign of the plane.

That was when she looked around and realized that her problems had only began. The Red Center stretched out all around her, an unbroken expanse of sunburned sand and grit as far as she could see. There were no trees, no buildings, no life at all. Only a few small hills and some largish rocks here and there interrupted the flat, featureless landscape. Looking around, Sydney understood why some people compared this part of the outback to the surface of Mars.

Sydney's heart sank as she realized what it meant to be stranded in such an utterly inhospitable spot. She was totally alone—except, presumably, for the unfortunate Rabik, though she could only hope with a shudder that she didn't stumble across whatever remained of him. She had no water, no food, and no idea which way led back to civilization. Even the position of the sun was no help to her: she didn't know whether it was midmorning or midafternoon, and even if she managed to figure it out in the next couple of hours by tracking the sun's movement across the sky, she still wouldn't know which direction she should be going. The outback was so immense that even if Noah knew she was somewhere out there, he could spend a month searching from the air and not even come close to finding her. And she had no way of contacting him or anyone else—unless her fingernail signaling device happened to work.

Lifting her hand, she stared down at the rhinestone still embedded in her thumbnail. What exactly had Graham said about it, anyway? The hot sun beating down on her and reflecting off the red sand was already making her feel a little light-headed and woozy. Focusing as best she could, she struggled to pull the conversation out of her memory.

"It's brand-new," Graham had explained eagerly. "Very high-tech stuff here, the smallest we've been able to get one of these yet. That's really the challenge for us most of the time, you know. We can do all sorts of cool stuff, technologically speaking, you know, but it's really not going to do you much good to have, say, a satellite signal interrupter that's the size of the whole satellite, or a digitally enhanced night-vision scope that you have to carry around in a wheelbarr—"

"Graham!" Sloane had interrupted sharply.

Graham had looked slightly flustered. "Oh, sorry," he'd blurted out. "Anyway, my point is, it's very new—in fact, we're still testing it. We know it's good up to a distance of fifty miles or so. That's in the city—it would probably go at least twice that out in a more open area, or even a forest or something. Or possibly way more than that. We just don't know yet. In fact, if you do use it, try to notice how far away you are from each other at the time, will you? It would really be helpful if we—"

Sloane had cut him off again at that point, and the meeting had moved on to other topics. Sydney bit her lip, still staring at the rhinestone and wondering exactly how much distance might be covered by Graham's "way more."

Then she shrugged. Either the signal would reach Noah, wherever he was, or it wouldn't. What did she have to lose?

She flicked open the rhinestone with a different fingernail, then pressed the tiny button that popped up.

Once that was done, she looked around again. Her throat was already feeling scratchy and dry with thirst, but she ignored it. Spotting the parachute lying limply nearby, she walked over and crouched beside it. She wished she still had her riding crop blade, but instead she was going to have to make do with a sharp-edged rock.

Starting at the edge of the chute, she began to saw at it with her makeshift knife. The fabric was lightweight but surprisingly tough, and it was only a matter of seconds before Sydney was sweating from the effort of cutting through it.

She was tempted to give up on the task. But she knew that the sun overhead was going to be one of her worst enemies—she could already feel the exposed skin of her face and arms baking in its strong rays, and she guessed that the air temperature was well over one hundred degrees. Her feet were sweating profusely in the leather riding boots, and she was tempted to rip them off . . . until she remembered that Australia was home to numerous species of highly venomous snakes and spiders.

Finally she managed to cut and tear loose a sizable, roughly circular piece of the parachute fabric. She slipped off her camera belt and tied the fabric to it, then strapped the belt onto her head, pouffing out the fabric so that it shaded her face, her neck, and part of her torso.

"Good enough," she muttered, though she still had to squint against the light reflecting off the sand.

She glanced upward again, trying to guess which direction was which. But once again, she decided it didn't matter much. Glancing at the remains of the parachute, she wondered if she should just stay put, maybe rig some kind of tent out of the parachute and hope that someone spotted it from the air and came to her rescue.

But she couldn't stand the thought of just sitting still and waiting for the intense heat or dehydration to finish her off. She had to do something, to keep moving as long as she could.

She picked a direction and started walking.

15

SYDNEY WASN'T SURE HOW long she'd been walking when she stopped to rest, dropping onto the sand and leaning against a large, reddish-gray boulder. Time seemed to be melting here beneath the hot, relentless onslaught of the sun, and the minutes—hours?—floated past in fits and starts. She was still wearing her watch, but its face had been smashed at some unknown point after the moment she'd jumped onto that horse back in Sydney.

She stared blankly at a patch of scrub grass, then let her eyes drift shut. That wild ride over the cross-country course seemed so long ago now. . . .

Sydney caught herself with a jerk, realizing she was drifting on the edge of sleep. The panic caused by that thought set her heart pumping a little more strongly and gave her the energy to sit up straight, causing several flies that had landed on her face to buzz angrily into the air. If she fell asleep now, she would have no chance at all.

Then again, did she have a chance to begin with? Things looked pretty hopeless. Sydney glanced around, hoping to see something—any-thing—different on the horizon ahead. But aside from a few more rocks here and there, and what ap-peared to be the sun-bleached skull of a longhorn cow about fifty yards away, there was nothing but mile upon mile of red sand.

She stared at the cow skull, mesmerized by the gleaming surface of its long, curved horns. Sud-denly she noticed a ribcage, presumably from the same cow, lying on the sand a few yards beyond the skull.

Is that the same cow skeleton I saw a while ago? she wondered dully, the image of a similar pile of bones floating vaguely through her mind. She shook her head. *No, it can't be. It must be a different one. Unless I'm walking in circles . . .*

In some part of her mind, she knew that she wouldn't be able to go on much longer before the outback overcame her. Nothing in her training had prepared her for this—nothing *could* have prepared her. Her knowledge of languages and codes, her talent for adopting a new alias, her fighting skills—the Krav Maga, the weapons training—none of it mattered here. All that mattered was the sun and the sand and the slow drip of time passing, silent and inexorable, as it had done for millennia.

The knowledge of her own almost inevitable fate—the image of her own bones baking there beneath the merciless sun alongside the remains of that unfortunate cow—beat against the inside of her own skull, throbbing in her mind with a rhythmic, relentless rumble that quickly grew to fill her entire body. Even the ground seemed to vibrate with it. For one delirious moment Sydney was certain that it was the sound of the red desert yawning open beneath her to swallow her whole.

Suddenly a shadow passed over her, startling her out of her daze, and she realized that the rhythmic thumping sound wasn't coming from inside her own head after all but from somewhere overhead. Waving away a fly and glancing up, she saw a helicopter banking overhead.

"Noah?" she mumbled from between parched, cracked lips.

As the helicopter swooped lower, some still-functioning sliver of logic in her mind recognized that it probably wasn't her partner coming to rescue her. Noah would have no way of finding her here—not unless that signaling device had worked a miracle. On the other hand, there were certain people who would know just where to look for her . . .

The steady thumping of the chopper blades came closer. Sydney weakly flung herself to the sand and rolled behind the boulder she'd been leaning against, though she knew it wouldn't offer much cover.

Before long the helicopter touched down on the red sand about a hundred yards from Sydney, and its blades slowed to a stop. Sydney peered out at it, her mind still and empty as she waited to see who would emerge.

The door opened and a dog leaped out, followed by another. Sydney stared at the pair of German shepherds sniffing around with interest at the sun-baked ground, wondering if her mind had finally given out for good.

Then again, they're training dogs to do some pretty amazing stuff these days, she thought giddily. *If they can teach a dog to sniff out plastic explosives, I don't see why one couldn't learn to fly a helicopter. . . .*

The goofy line of thought ended abruptly as a

man climbed out of the helicopter after the dogs, holding the ends of their long leashes, which Sydney hadn't even noticed at this distance. Sydney hadn't thought she had the energy left to be frightened, but as she recognized the bulky form and cruel face, she felt her hands start shaking. It was Lawton.

"Steady, gentlemen," Lawton said to the dogs, his low voice drifting to Sydney through the hot, silent air. "Just give me a second here."

Sydney squinted, trying to see what Lawton was doing as he shifted both leashes to one hand and fiddled with something he was holding in the other. It looked like a cell phone or other small electronic device.

Whatever it was, it gave out a loud series of beeps. The dogs glanced around alertly at the sound, wagging their tails, and Lawton smiled.

"Ah," he said loudly. "It seems our quarry might be even closer than I thought. All right, gentlemen—have a whiff."

Sydney saw him pull a small piece of fabric out of his pocket and hold it in front of the dogs. They sniffed it, then barked, straining at the ends of their leashes.

Realizing that it would be only a matter of seconds before the dogs found her, Sydney glanced around wildly. There was no other significant cover anywhere in sight. Feeling desperate, trapped in the total openness of the desert, she wondered if it might be possible to crawl to the cow skeleton, maybe fight them off with one of the ribs. . . . But even as she tried to calculate how long it would take her to reach the skull or the piles of bones beyond, she heard the dogs' barks coming rapidly closer.

She tried to pull her weak, dehydrated muscles into some semblance of a fighting stance. A second later the dogs leaped around the rock and stopped in front of her, their tails wagging as they barked triumphantly.

"Ah, there you are, Miss Bristow." Lawton, still holding the leashes, stepped around the boulder and smiled down at her with a wicked gleam in his dark eyes. Those eyes scanned her slowly, taking in her sunburned skin, ripped clothes, and haggard expression. "However, I see I needn't have made the trip after all—the outback was about to finish you off for me." His smile widened. "But then, that would have denied me the pleasure of killing you myself."

Beneath Lawton's smile and the jovial voice, Sydney sensed a chilling fury. "Wh-why?" she panted, unable to manage any more.

"Why?" Lawton repeated. "Why do I want to

kill you, you mean?" His smile faded. "You're not an idiot, Miss Bristow. I know who you work for—and I know that you and your partner have surely already mucked up my little scheme here. That's reason enough for me to want you gone. But then . . ." He paused, almost shaking with anger. The dogs whined anxiously, looking up at him. "Then you go and send my daughter to hospital."

Sydney blinked, confused. "Are you talking about Melanie's fall on course?" she mumbled. "But I didn't—"

"Luckily she's going to be all right," Lawton interrupted sharply. "If she weren't . . ." He paused again, longer this time, as a whole rainbow of emotions played over his face. "Well, let's just say if that were that the case, you'd be praying that I'd left you to die alone in the Never Never." He took a deep breath, and the tight smile returned. "But no worries. I'll see that your death is quick and merciful. At least sort of."

Sydney realized that he blamed her for his daughter's fall. *He didn't know about the trip wire,* she thought dully, pulling her foot back as one of the dogs sniffed at it. *Rabik must've rigged that up on his own because he wanted an excuse to snag Chipper. That must be the gray he kept talking about that Lawton wouldn't let them take.*

Even as that last piece of the puzzle was snapping into place, another part of her mind was still wondering at Lawton's devotion to his daughter. In a man involved in Lawton's line of work, such a relationship could certainly be seen as a weakness. But Sydney found it both touching and disconcerting. Would her own father ever think of avenging her if the opportunity presented itself? Would he even feel a twinge of ill will toward her killer? She grimaced, already sure of the answer.

"Nothing to say for yourself?" Lawton shrugged. "All right, let's go on and get this over with, then."

He turned away for a moment, tugging on the dogs' leashes. Leading them over to the helicopter, he quickly tied the dogs to one of the base supports. They immediately crawled under the shade cast by the chopper's belly and flopped down on the sand, panting.

As Lawton walked back toward her, flexing his fingers, Sydney tried to push herself to a standing position. But her weak limbs betrayed her, and she fell back against the boulder, banging her hip painfully. By the time she glanced up again, Lawton was standing in front of her.

"I know I said this would be quick," he commented, his tone as calm and casual as if he were discussing the weather back in his own wood-paneled den. "But not *too* quick. I want to feel the life going out of you myself—that way I'll know you're out of my hair for good."

Sydney breathed heavily, still exhausted from her efforts to stand. So he meant to strangle her—if she could gather her energy again, maybe she could still get the better of him somehow. Maybe her training would kick in. She knew it was a long shot, but it was the only shot she had.

But it meant she had to keep him talking. At the moment, she didn't even have the strength to fight off the flies that kept landing on her face and trying to crawl up her nose. Feeling like a character on a bad mystery show, she cleared her throat, which was dry and scratchy. "How—how did you find me?" she croaked.

Lawton chuckled. "Not quite ready to go yet after all, eh?" he said. "All right then, I suppose you have a right to a last chat. Just don't go and die on me in the meantime and take away my fun, okay?"

Sydney glared at him. He grinned in return. She shuddered slightly as she realized that he really *was* having fun. How could such an evil man have fathered a person as nice as Melanie?

"When my boys radioed me from the plane, they seemed to think you'd certainly been killed when you took that dive—you and that clumsy fool

Rabik." His face twisted into a scowl for a moment. "Bloody bludger. Never did trust him anyhow."

Sydney wanted to tell him he'd had good reason for that, wanted to let him in on Rabik's trip-wire plan. But she was just too exhausted. Besides, what was the point? She remained silent as Lawton went on.

"But they also mentioned you'd taken one of the parachutes with you, and I know SD-6 doesn't train their agents to die if there's any way around it. So I figured I'd best check around, make sure you really were a splat on the sand somewhere. I hopped in my chopper and buzzed up to the spot where they said they'd dropped you—luckily it wasn't too far in. I was checking the area for signs of that parachute when one of my scanners picked up a signal. It wasn't any of the known locals, so I figured it had to be you trying to call for help."

Sydney's eyes fluttered shut. The fingernail device. Instead of summoning Noah to her rescue, it had showed Lawton exactly where to find her.

Never mind, she thought wearily, opening her eyes again. *He would have spotted the parachute and tracked me down anyway. This just helped him get here a little faster.*

Meanwhile Lawton was fishing in his pants pocket. He pulled out the scrap of cloth he'd shown the dogs. "Luckily I happened to have your scent on my chair cushions back home. I'd grabbed it on my way out, along with my furry mates there." He gestured toward the dogs, who were still resting in the shadow of the helicopter. "So I picked a likely spot and landed, figuring they'd lead me to you soon enough, and got very lucky."

He cracked his knuckles and took another step toward her. His smile was gone, replaced by a grim, focused expression that told Sydney he wasn't going to be distracted by any more chitchat. He loomed over her, his bulk temporarily blocking the glare of the sun in her eyes.

"Time to say good-bye, Miss Bristow," he murmured, reaching toward her.

Sydney gathered her strength and struck out, knocking his hands away. Shoving herself off the boulder for leverage, she managed to stagger to her feet.

She ran toward the helicopter, stumbling in the sand but somehow remaining upright. The dogs, noticing that something was happening, crawled out from under the chopper and started barking, pulling at their leashes. Sydney veered away, realizing that she wouldn't be able to get past them. So much for her vague plan of flying off in the chopper. . . .

"Hey!" Lawton's voice was very close behind her. He sounded more annoyed than angry. "What's wrong with you? You're only making things harder on yourself."

Sydney didn't dare look back. She just ran past the helicopter, not really knowing what she was doing. Every step sapped more of her dwindling supply of strength. But she couldn't stop. Keeping her eyes on the horizon, she staggered on—another step, and another . . .

Her foot hit something half-buried in the sand and she tripped, her body thudding heavily onto the ground. The air whooshed out of her body, leaving her limp. Rolling painfully onto her side, she found herself staring straight into the empty eye sockets of the cow skull.

Lawton ran up beside her a second later, breathing heavily in the oppressive, dry heat. "Are you a total whacker?" he panted. He kicked her hard in the side, sending her flying onto her back beside the bleached skull. "You're really just dragging things out, you know. Now hold still, and let's finish this off. I promised Mel I'd be there for visiting hours, and time's running short."

Sydney sprawled where she'd landed, feeling the smooth but oddly gritty surface of the skull against one arm and the heat of the sand prickling against her back. All of her adrenaline was gone, leaving her as empty and hopeless as she'd ever been in her life. He was right. There was a point beyond which it was useless to fight. She might as well give up and accept her fate. Who would miss her, really? SD-6 would find another agent to take her place. Francie would be sad for a while, but she had so many other friends; she would be fine. Her father barely acknowledged her existence as it was. But Noah . . .

A tear seeped out of her eye as Sydney's thoughts flipflopped from what she had with Noah to her father's dour, emotionless face. She would never see either of them again.

Lawton leaned over her, straddling her prone body as he reached down toward her neck. "There, that's better," he panted. "Now we'll just— *Aargh!*"

He cried out, startled, as Sydney called upon her last reserves of strength and kicked her legs sharply sideways, knocking him off balance. At the same time she grabbed his arm and, using his own weight and bulk against him, flipped him over to one side—directly onto the long, sharp, gleaming horns of the cow skull.

Lawton gave one last, strangled yell, then a few burbling gasps. Then there was only silence.

Sydney lay there for a moment, her eyes closed.

Her body relaxed as several minutes passed with no sounds of life other than the frantic barking of the dogs back at the helicopter.

Finally summoning the energy to open her eyes, she looked over at Lawton—and quickly looked away. He was dead, the red of his blood seeping into the red sand beneath him.

But her relief didn't last long as she realized that she would soon be just as dead herself. She wondered if there was water in the helicopter. If she could get to it, maybe she could even fly herself to safety. Of course, she would have to get past those dogs first. . . .

She tried to move, to push herself upright. But her last efforts had sapped any strength she had left, and her body refused to obey. Her mind wasn't behaving much better—as she looked at her own arm, the air around it seemed to swim and wriggle, transforming into a hundred dancing wormlike shapes that appeared to cling to her skin. She shook her head, trying to clear it of the psychedelic aura closing in at the edges of her vision and joining with the dancing worms until she couldn't see straight.

I can't give up, she told herself fiercely. *I can't. That's not who I am!*

But even the thought of dragging herself the

thirty yards or so to the helicopter filled her with such utter exhaustion that it was hard to breathe. She tried to look over at the chopper, to gauge the distance and the dogs' moods. But all she could see was a vast, yawning pit that had suddenly opened up between herself and her goal. It was a seething, worm-filled chasm of black nothingness, and it was rushing closer to her with every passing second.

It was very tempting to allow herself to slide into that darkness. But just as she was about to give in, she heard a new sound above the yaps of the dogs—a steady thrumming from somewhere over-head. Her eyes flew open, and she scanned the sky. Dots and swirls of color crowded her vision, but through them she saw a solid, dark shape overhead. It was another helicopter.

Sydney squinted up at it, trying to figure out whether it was real or just another product of her delirium. Her head cleared slightly as the sound of the chopper blades came closer, filling her ears. The dogs were barking again, but she could hardly hear them over the noise as the chopper veered down-ward and settled onto the sand a short distance from the first one.

She couldn't fight anymore. Sydney knew that with every fiber of her being. If more enemies climbed out of the chopper, she was done for.

The door opened. Sydney blinked, wondering if she was seeing things again. That couldn't really be Noah climbing out, could it?

"It's her!" his familiar voice floated over the sand as he turned and gestured to someone else within the helicopter. "She's right over here!"

Noah leaped to the sand and ran toward her. Just behind him, a pair of men in white medics' uniforms climbed out of the chopper carrying a lightweight stretcher.

"Syd!" Noah cried, skidding to his knees beside her. "Are you still with us?"

He grabbed her hand. She squeezed back, noticing how cool and moist his skin felt.

"I'm still here," she whispered hoarsely.

Still clinging to his hand, she finally let herself relax and slide into unconsciousness.

16

"SO DOES THIS MEAN you and your dad are going to, like, hang out more now?" Francie asked, glancing up from painting her toenails a shocking shade of orange. She was sitting on her rumpled bed in their dorm room in her nightgown. The midmorning sunshine was pouring through the open window, and the sounds of students hurrying to or from class floated in from outside.

Sydney shrugged, using the laundry she was folding on her bed as an excuse not to meet her friend's eyes. She had decided to blow off her morning classes, and was still in her pajamas and robe. It had been almost a week since her rescue from the outback, but she still felt drained most of the time, no matter how much she slept. The doctors in Australia had told her that would be the case—and that she was lucky she would suffer no permanent damage from her battle with the elements.

"Um, I don't know," she mumbled. "I mean, yeah, he wanted me there when he was sick. But we've still got that history. . . ."

Francie gave her a sharp, concerned glance. "Right," she said. "But don't you think this might be your chance to move past that? I mean, not that I can tell you what to do, of course. But I'd hate to see you waste an opportunity to make things better, you know? He *is* still your dad."

"I know."

Sydney had returned to school just the evening before. Francie had taken pity on her obvious exhaustion at first and hadn't asked too many questions. Sydney had explained that her bruised face was the result of a slip on the stairs at her father's house, and her sunburned skin had come from a foolish sunscreen oversight.

But this morning Francie seemed all too eager to explore Sydney's relationship with her father, which happened to be one of the last things Sydney wanted to think about. She was still suffering from periodic flashes of guilt about killing Lawton. She had been trained to kill—that was part of life as a CIA agent, and the part of her job she disliked the most.

Despite Lawton's many flaws, she knew without a doubt that Melanie had loved him, and that he had adored her in return. She was sure that back in Australia right now Melanie was absolutely devastated, and that she would probably never know just what kind of man her father had been or how he had really died. It just seemed like a waste somehow.

"Look, we don't have to talk about this right now if you're not up for it," Francie said after a moment of silence. "But I'm here for you, okay?"

Sydney forced what she hoped looked like a sincere smile. "I know," she told Francie. "Thanks for caring. Really."

Francie returned the smile. "No problem," she said. "Hey, I'm starved. After my tootsies dry, want to go grab some breakfast burritos or something?" She wriggled her newly painted toenails eagerly.

Sydney hesitated. The last thing she wanted to do was go out and face the buzz of everyday life right then. But she didn't want to hurt Francie's feelings by saying no.

She was relieved when the sharp buzz of her

pager interrupted. "Oops, better get that," she said apologetically.

Grabbing the pager from her bedside table, she saw that it was Sloane. For once, she was happy to have an excuse to escape from campus for a while. It just felt a little too soon to go back to what she used to think of as real life.

"Sorry. I've got to go." She jumped to her feet and started pulling on her jeans under her robe. "There's probably a ton of work to make up at the bank since I was gone so long."

A split second of irritation passed over Francie's face, but then she shrugged. "Sure," she said with just a hint of a sigh. "I understand. I'll just have to make it burritos for one."

* * *

Half an hour later Sydney was hurrying down the hall on her way to Sloane's office. As she rounded a corner, she saw Noah leaning against the wall and stopped short.

He straightened up. "Hey," he greeted her. "Figured you'd be here soon."

"Here I am," Sydney said. "I'm due in Sloane's office."

Her mind raced. She hadn't had much chance

to talk with Noah since he'd flown in to rescue her. At the hospital in Sydney, there had always been other people around. And Noah had flown back to the States a couple of days earlier than she had.

Noah fell into step beside her as she walked on down the hall. "Congratulations," he said with a tentative smile. "You're a hero around here, you know. Those microchips you snagged on the plane turned out to be major stuff."

"Really? That's good." Sydney didn't want to admit that she barely remembered pocketing the chips. That whole day was still a bit of a blur, though certain details stood out in sharp relief— leaping over that hot dog cart on Chipper, her midair struggle with Rabik, and of course, Lawton's final, gurgling breaths as he lay beside her on the red sand.

Noah nodded, shoving his hands deep into his pockets as he walked. "Sloane is very pleased," he said. "You'll win big points for this one, Syd." He cast her a sidelong glance and winked. "And I hope I win some points from you—you know, for swooping in just in the nick of time. It's lucky I was already searching for you at Lawton's place. When I saw him take off in that helicopter with the dogs, I decided I'd better see where he was going in such a hurry."

"So what took you so long to get there?" Sydney joked weakly.

Noah answered her question seriously. "In hindsight, I wish I'd stuck a little closer to him," he said. "But at the time, I didn't want him to even suspect he was being followed." He shrugged and grinned. "Besides, it took me a while to get used to flying on the wrong side of the road."

Sydney smiled at the lame joke. "Well, I'm just glad you found me," she said. She stopped and turned to face him in the empty hallway. "In case I didn't say it back at the hospital—thanks."

Noah met her eyes. "You're welcome," he said huskily.

There was a long moment of silence as they just looked at each other. Sydney thought she would never get tired of staring into the endless depths of his eyes, of examining every craggy detail of his ruggedly handsome face.

Finally Noah laughed shortly and tore his eyes away, shattering the moment. "Anyway, I guess we're even now," he said.

"Huh?" Sydney blinked, still a little confused by that intense look they'd just shared and not sure what he was talking about for a moment.

Noah turned and started walking again, glancing over at her briefly as he answered. "You know," he said. "You pointed out how you saved me in Paris. I guess I never paid you back properly for that, our recent jaunt last month in Amsterdam notwithstanding. I owed you one."

Sydney smiled weakly. "Right," she said.

She didn't say anything else about it since they'd just reached Sloane's office. Inside, she could see Sloane, Graham, and several others already seated and waiting for the meeting to start.

But at Noah's words, she had just realized something important.

Noah and I will probably always be sort of competitive with each other, she thought. *That's just human nature—well, the nature of these particular humans, anyway. But the truth is, there's really no point in keeping score.*

Just then Sloane looked up and saw her. His eyes crinkled at the corners as he smiled at her. "Sydney!" he called in his most jovial voice. "Welcome back. Ah, and Agent Hicks is with you. Good, good. Come on in, you two, and let's get started."

Sydney glanced at Noah as he gestured for her to precede him into the room. Nodding her thanks, she stepped over the threshold.

In our line of work, she thought, *we just do what we have to.*